"Peopled by gay and straight men and women exiled within the human heart, this lexical tour de force . . . embraces midnight storms and morning calm, humor and pain, Puerto Rican heat and cold Chicago wind. By the end of this book, you'll be naked enough to feel the green sparks of another body beside you in the darkened room."
—Maurice Kilwein Guevara

"With this startling collection of stories, Rane Arroyo has proven that he can write just about anything. At turns lyrical, bracing and even experimental, these varied fictions cement Arroyo's place at the absolute forefront of Latino literature in America today. Highly recommended." **—Luis Urrea**

"Hauntingly beautiful; tender as a sharp knife poised at the heart. Rane Arroyo's visions make you want to kneel on a bed of roses and pray for redemption." **Lawrence La Fountain Stokes**

"These compelling stories track the complexity of having to navigate through the storm of sexual, cultural, and social identity—indeed, a violent yet beautiful hurricane without a name, but with the vibrant voice of Arroyo's characters who weather the storm with utmost dignity and grace." **—Richard Blanco**

"The publication of *How to Name a Hurricane* is cause for celebration. Here's a writer at the peak of his creative powers, letting loose, delving deep not only into his heart and spirit, but his life as a gay Latino in the United States. This is a brave, honest book, well orchestrated and executed. Mr. Arroyo, in this sweet concoction of stories and poems, has masterfully created a gem of a book and a riveting read." **—Virgil Suarez**

HOW TO NAME A HURRICANE

Camino del Sol

A LATINA AND LATINO LITERARY SERIES

How to Name a Hurricane

RANE ARROYO

THE UNIVERSITY OF ARIZONA PRESS TUCSON

The University of Arizona Press

∞ This book is printed on acid-free, archival-quality paper.

Manufactured in the United States of America
10 09 08 07 06 05 6 5 4 3 2 1

Library of Congress Cataloging-in-Publication Data
Arroyo, Rane.
How to name a hurricane / Rane Arroyo.
p. cm. — (Camino del sol)
ISBN-13: 978-0-8165-2460-0 (pbk. : acid-free paper)
ISBN-10: 0-8165-2460-2 (pbk. : acid-free paper)
I. Title. II. Series.
PS3551.R722H69 2005
818'.5409—dc22

2004029225

Publication of this book is made possible in part by the proceeds of a permanent endowment created with the assistance of a Challenge Grant from the National Endowment for the Humanities, a federal agency.

Dedicated to Glenn and the Bee

to Uncle Rachel

Also to my mentors: Jean Genet,

Italo Calvino, Yasunari Kawabata,

James Baldwin,

and Reinaldo Arenas

Introduction

THE NAKED VENTRILOQUIST

Beware a naked ventriloquist.

This is a book of voices. When I went to the gay clubs in the 1980s, I was struck by the fact that upon entering dark refuges from heterosexuality, many of our daily markers had been erased or altered: there were no clocks, many of the windows had been painted over and the music throbbed and was so loud that the only talking we could do was on the dance floors when we writhed and owned our blue midnights. The irony was that by being fictitious to each other we often moved closer and closer to personal and universal truths.

Here is a collection of short stories, monologues, a long story told in verse, and/or purgatorial tales. In other words, this is a collection of fictions. While I'm primarily known as a poet and playwright, I have been publishing prose throughout my career. I have only now gathered it in one collection. I think of it as a storm that has been gaining strength, drop by drop by drop, from 1993 to 2005.

Why all these genre crossings with short stories that vary from the traditional to one that imitates the verse numbers of the Christian Bible to a longer work in which the narrative is picked up by a sudden shift in viewpoint but all told from the first person voice(s)? Certainly I have been long aware, and have anticipated, the inevitable packaging of gay identity by corporations. While many of us can share iconic figures and historical events (such as Stonewall, AIDS when it was first GRID, Ricky Martin's first scene-stealing Grammy performance, etc.), many of us have had to invent our lives. When I first read Jean Genet, Gertrude Stein, Federíco García Lorca, Reinaldo Arenas, Jean Cocteau, James Baldwin, and so many others, I learned from them that the marginalized writer must achieve at least three simultaneous goals: (1) shatter the restrictions of a genre, (2) work in multiple genres, and (3) cull the dislocations that only the exile, whether exterior or interior, comes to know intimately.

Instead of opting for simple narratives, I have decided to trust the intelligence of my international readers. These fictions, then, are evidence that I, and so many others, are still defining ourselves as the complex communities of same-sex lovers who are also citizens, daughters and sons, neighbors, human beings. Add my Latino identity, working class identity, educational journey, a writer's relentless obstacles (both interior and exterior), the fifty addresses of houses in which I have lived so far, my Midwest soul, and my careers as teacher, waiter, temporary worker, factory worker, banker, secretary, and, finally, writer—it's a mess; it's chaos; it's an opportunity to speak from multiple positionalities.

Notice how (deliberately) there is an "I" in this introduction and within all the fictions being shared in this collection. Beyond the incredible gift of humans having empathy to each other, "I" is also an elusive prey and/or reward. As I began conceiving of gathering these voices into one book, there was one layover at an airport in which I found myself telling a stranger some of the stories of my life that I hadn't yet shared with many of my friends, readers and colleagues. Why was I willing to trust someone who I just met with so many of my secrets?

This is the tone I offer in these fictions—not as confessional works or exercises in mimesis. I was and continue to be intrigued by *intimacy*: that talk with the man on the barstool next to you before last call after you both admit that you don't want to sleep with each other and yet it feels good to have a temporary best friend; that talk between two Latinos at a conference clinging to each other and meaning to e-mail each other but don't; that talk after waking up next to a stranger and grinning before the day returns you both to the responsibilities that suddenly feel like someone else's debts.

The writers mentioned in my dedication taught me when no one else thought me worthy of attention; the library card, to me, is the most magical and dangerous power in the United States. Why aren't librarians treated as the visionaries they often are? They know, as I do, that voices stay with a reader long after a book is closed (consumption being the assumption). Unlike echoes, these voices rarely fade away.

These fictions cross genres as they must in order to capture the lives of gay Latinos as we make sense and make nonsense of the chaos that surrounds us. So many of us have been ignored. Some of us have not survived. I have devoted my writing career to be inclusive of men and women I have met in my life's journey. While our sorrows matter, so do the times of joy, the times of dancing, daydreaming, pettiness, political fury and all moments that are easily lost if not captured. I'm still struck by the fact that no one can simply share photographs without commenting or elaborating upon the images. Stories must always be more than about mere documentation. The mind is attracted to music, imagination, puzzles, and opportunities for empathy.

Beware. Meeting someone can change the universe, and/or, finally reveal it.

I have been naked and I have been a ventriloquist. When I have been both at the same time, there has been both enjoyment in the theatricality of sex and the fear that I may be too successful at avoiding love. There is more to me, and to everyone I know, than meets the eye, than meets the "I."

But tell me one thing—tell me honestly:

Have you heard word of where my son lives?

HOMER, *THE ODYSSEY,* BOOK 11: 35–36

Johnny, why don't you remember me?

JIMMY SOMERVILLE WITH BRONSKI BEAT, "I FEEL LOVE,"

THE SINGLES COLLECTION 1984–1990.

My Blue Midnights

My ears are ringing so I can't help but think my family is already talking about me.

I don't think I'm that interesting once I get out of other people's beds.

The country of my bed is only for invited tourists.

I stop at *Little Jim's* for a drink before I go to the family party for another cousin who is engaged.

It's only 4 o'clock in a Gemini afternoon but already the bar is crowded.

I see lots of businessmen eyeing unemployed (or unemployable, as my friend Linc insists) men in cowboy suits.

How has the gay world become so full of uniforms?

A younger man nonchalantly stares at me.

I look away and see one of the suits staring at him.

In the beginning was the triangle and it is still holy.

I walk over to the jukebox to see if there are any new Spanish songs on there and I find the same old one: "Feliz Navidad."

Jesus, why is there a Christmas song on this jukebox in the middle of June?

I swallow my warm Budweiser and hurry out of the bar before I have to reject a skinny man with an eye patch who is seeking rejection, and probably wouldn't believe that I'm late for a family party.

It's so strange but the inside of a gay bar is like being inside an imaginary country; rarely are there clocks nor even clues to which city you might be in.

It's a no-man's land filled with men.

It's as if we're all amnesiacs without any other IDs other than what hangs between our legs.

I'm an exile who isn't an exile.

I think of my parents arriving in Chicago not knowing any words of English, their Puerto Rico becoming only Puerto Pobre.

How they used to bundle us up in the winters as if we were going out to play in a new ice age.

When put to bed, we were dressed like lumberjacks in case we were secret sleepwalkers.

I guess I'll never be the sexy narcoleptic that River Phoenix played in *My Own Private Idaho*.

My boots hit the sidewalks in a regular rhythm and I think of that song that Uncle Diego, before he became Uncle Linda, used to sing: *There is a rose / that grows / in Spanish Harlem*.

I arrive at the party, take a deep breath and ring the doorbell.

The cousin, who is pregnant and fifteen, is being honored for trapping her man, an electrician who is even in a union.

She shrugs at me and cousin Tony embraces me while pushing me into the living room.

He is one of the family's heroes because he has been a rich banker's (I've never seen a poor banker) personal chauffeur for over ten years.

Tony's tragedy is that he hasn't had enough free time to make children, or at least "legal ones" as Mami whispered to me at another party for another pregnant cousin.

In our family, sometimes we have celebrations to celebrate the fact that nothing bad has happened in a long time.

Tony's wife, Rosa, kisses me on the cheek and sighs, "Ricky, you've finally got here. It's you and me against them. I've been doing my part."

It's a well-established, if undiscussed fact in the family, that I don't have children either.

Rosa finds this a more important link than I do, but it provides me an entry, or reentry, into the family often enough.

Bells cut out of white tissue paper are taped everywhere so it feels like I'm inside a church just for albinos.

My secret life is no secret anymore.

It's supposed to be my secret love.

Where is he?

Will I never sing: *eres tú / la agua de mi. . . .*?

Cousin Blanca walks into the living room, her body stuffed into a white Christian Dior yacht-dress and rushes forward to embrace me.

"I told your mother this morning you would show up," she purrs. "Your parents told me that you wouldn't. That you had to go to the ballet or something that you—you know—you like to do."

"I like to do everything," I smile back. "That's how I get in trouble."

Rosa chokes and Blanca beams.

Sometimes I wish either of these women had been my mother.

"Where are Mami and Papi?" I ask.

"They'll be here. You know your mother. She's like a daughter of the tides. She leaves the suburbs when there isn't any traffic. She wasn't that nervous when she was young. But who is young anymore? Not even you. I see gray hairs, hijo."

"That's because I am very good on some very bad nights." I feel drunk, strangely happy.

I like the sound of Spanish and English filling the room.

Some of the men are huddled, talking about the Cubs vs. the White Socks, that ancient argument where it's been agreed there are no clear-cut winners.

I join the women in the kitchen who are never more than a few steps away from the liquor.

I grab a beer, look at it in case it's on the latest boycott list—it's not!

Blanca hits my hand. "Put that back, you barbarian. I have a surprise for you."

She pushes me through the hallway into the dining room where a bar has been set up. "See something you like?"

I follow her gaze and see a handsome bartender. "Blanca, are you trying to get me in trouble?"

"Let's just say I'm trying to manage the trouble you're already in."

Jesus, I have a sudden taste for a cigarette even though I don't really smoke except when I'm drunk or nervous or sexed-out.

I rarely smoke.

Blanca leans forward. "Haven't you had enough of this business? Your parents making up excuses. You never join the family because your parents. . . ."

I kiss her. "Is this like a late graduation present?"

"It's up to you to make it a party. I know it's a fact the stud is suffering from a broken heart. So just keep it below the waist, you get me, huh? You'd be surprised what can crawl from down there to up here." She pounds her chest and then dramatically winks before walking away.

I savor the moment.

I feel as if I'm in *Brideshead Revisited*, but with a mambo soundtrack.

"Hola, hermano." I'm a fucking idiot, I think to myself.

Why am I calling such a stud my brother?

The bartender smiles back. "Are you my tip?"

I pull back. "What do you mean?"

"You're the Ricky that Blanca told me about."

I nod, "The little that she knows to tell you."

He extends his hand, "I'm Pablo."

I hold his hand, "And I'm very happy that you are Pablo."

He breaks into a smile. "Ah, they warned me that you could be charming and that you have a fat bank account."

I smile back. "This is going to sound crazy, but I feel happy today. I mean, just being with my family—look at these criminals. You're. . . here and I'm. . . ."

"Also . . . happy."

"Right," I wink back. "Happy."

"But you haven't asked me about my broken heart!"

"Tell me about your broken heart," I ask while trying to offer my best *GQ* scowl.

Pablo gestures toward a drink, "You're too sober and I'm working."

"Can I ask just one thing?"

"As long as it's not the kind of question that is too inspirational."

I lean forward. "You sound like a Hallmark Card."

"What's your question?" Pablo asks as if he is guiding me back home through a billion mile journey. I like his tenderness.

"Was he Spanish or American."

"He was Spanish-American. A Latino. I only sleep with our kind. Who do you sleep with?"

The robot in me can't be stopped once again, "Usually myself."

Pablo puts his hand over mine. "Look, I've been hearing about you for nearly a month. And you are handsome. And you might even be sweet. I don't want to talk about me, OK? I want to talk about spending next summer in Madrid. Or some other adventure we might have, can have. Stupid, right?"

I cock my head, "Are you a professional bartender?"

He shrugs, "Ricky, I'm licensed. God, that makes me sound like James Bond, no? Did you see Rob Lowe, no wait, it was Tom Cruise in that terrible movie where he serves drinks in the Caribbean?"

"No, but I'll have to rent it now."

Rosa shows up. "Sorry to interrupt this—whatever it is—but I need your help. The uncles are arguing about who will be godfather to our children."

Pablo points, "You two . . .?"

I shake my head, "No, it's a joke. . . ."

Rosa yells, "We're two of a kind."

I'm dragged off into the living room.

I wave goodbye to Pablo and he waves back.

Forgive me this literary theft, but I'm surfing one of Virginia

Woolf's waves and drunk on adrenaline: the waves, the waves, and yet more waves.

Uncle Tony grabs me, "Am I or am I not your favorite uncle?"

I nod my head, "No."

Everyone laughs.

Uncle only pats me on my back, "America is still a land of choices, right?"

"Right," I laugh. "But you're always going to be my uncle. I have no choice!"

Uncle Tony playfully pushes me away and I watch as the conversation slowly descends into a series of private concerns and confessions.

I can't help but think of Uncle Linda and wonder what he is doing right now, at this very moment—no, wait—this very second, right now.

How many times I have tried to find him but it seems he has legally changed his last name too.

A transvestite in the family still has no place at the table during prayers for our god is a jealous god and wants the spotlight all to himself.

Ask me about Spanish men I admire and I'll tell you of my Uncle Linda, he who taught me how to dance to Aretha Franklin records, whose last words to me before he disappeared (lost desperadoes in America): *Honey, I'm taking a slow boat to China and I may never see you again but think of me each time you open a fortune cookie.*

Those were his last words.

Then he was gone.

I wonder if I'll disappear just like that someday.

I need a new drink, a new bartender.

Funny word—"bartender."

Tender bar.

Father Time, love me tender and I'll be so good to you too.

Maybe I'll even be good for you.

I think of escaping my family, of making my way back to *Little Jim's* and being picked up.

I want to be seduced tonight and not be the seducer.

I've been dismissed as a fucking romantic by many of my so-called amigos.

These thoughts get cut off because Mami and Papi arrive.

All too soon, I'm their referee once again.

I avoid Pablo, feeling as unsexy as an old bean burrito in a *7-11* microwave.

■ ■ ■

Eventually I do call Pablo and he meets me at the *Chicago Diner*, a trendy vegetarian restaurant blocks from the bars.

I'm a creature of habit, feeling safe only with the familiar, the explored, the tamed.

Christopher Columbus I am not.

I always have to know where the emergency exit is in the theater, the skyscraper, airplane and on first dates.

Little Jim's is two blocks from here and *French Kissing* is three.

Pablo shows up, looking a little older than he did at the party.

Perhaps that's because he is dressed more informally, in jeans and a tank top.

Or maybe I'm just sober.

We smile at each other, stumble through orders, and face each other without saying much of anything.

He breaks the silence. "So your lovers, Americans?"

I smile back, but not so to reveal much of anything. "You and I are Americans too."

Pablo laughs and the tension breaks.

I like this man, although I don't know if I can love this man.

Why am I thinking about this over lentil soup, with a side of hand-shredded carrots?

He says, “When I was young I wanted to change the colors of my eyes. I wanted them to be sea blue.”

I stare at his brown eyes, the eyes of a Mark Anthony before his encounter with a destiny nicknamed Egypt.

God, I have to stop reading personal ads.

I smile, “There are contacts for that now.”

Pablo shrugs. “But I’ve changed. I came to realize that blue eyes wouldn’t help me look like a James Dean wannabe.”

“I wanted to look like Sal Mineo, the smart one in *Rebel Without a Cause*.”

Pablo pats my hand. “At least, you picked a dark hero.”

“So what do you think?”

Pablo understands. He shakes his head. “It won’t work. You, hijo, are too Americanized to live in my world. You know your family’s party. Well, I belong there.”

“I don’t.”

Pablo plays at twirling his pretend mustache. “And someday you’ll succeed. And you’ll get away from them too.”

“What do you mean?”

“Ricky, I watched you watch them. I’m not even sure if you know how far away you’ve placed everyone from you.”

I must be crazy, but I just put my right hand in his crotch and rubbed him. “I’m right here, baby.”

Pablo lifts the hand, kisses the open palm and puts it gently into my own lap. “You’re too Puertorriqueño and no matter how you try, you can’t make the United States your real bed. I’m not talking about your body. I’m sure it knows how to sleep almost anywhere.”

There is a pause and we’re both laughing.

I feel so good.

I want to love this man.

“I want to love you, Pablo.”

“I want to love you too, Ricky, but . . . “

I stop him from talking.

The dinner is excellent as usual and deserving of the big tip I offer.

I walk Pablo to Belmont Avenue and flag down a taxi for him, but before he enters it I kiss him slowly on the lips.

His hands wrap around my hips.

He pulls me to him.

We can't let go.

We can't let go.

We don't let go.

I jump into the taxi and we go to his place near the *Taco Bell* in Andersonville.

We walk up the stairs past stoners in black T-shirts and underwear munching on tacos.

I think how the neighborhood looks like a Mexican Disneyland.

Pablo's apartment is crazier than I thought it would be because he seemed so damn polite and not the free spirit he feels free to be at home.

There are cacti painted on the wall; orange chairs are all over the place.

They're like pumpkins that no one will carve with human faces.

There are different colored lightbulbs in the lamps throughout his place.

Pablo has filled an aquarium with broken wine glasses.

"Souvenirs of parties?" I ask in an amused voice, "Or glass slippers you've refused?"

He gives me a look that makes him look like a brat, a mischievous little boy, a sideshow barker.

I thank Pablo for being my new brother, though I want and need him to be my lover.

I thank the men whose names I don't remember for giving me memories that I'll never forget.

We mess up his place as our shadows rub against each other.

Making love with him is both silly and beautiful.

His brown skin covers me and it feels like I'm falling into the sun head-first.

I wake up at midnight, my heart racing.

I look at the man next to me and Pablo looks uncannily like me; we're not twins, but we do look as if we come from the same planet.

I wake him up and insist we walk naked to his balcony.

"Los vecinos will call the cops, hombre," he half-protests.

"Fuck your neighbors," I growl.

"Dios, you're not going to be very faithful, are you, Ricky?"

He pulls me to him and soon I get him to look out at a city of lights.

Chicago, Chicago, Chicago.

We don't say anything.

We don't need to speak in Spanish or English about this moment as the weight of his body and mine are burdens we share.

Puerto Rico, my heart's devotion, let it sink back in the ocean.

I quote musicals at the worst times.

I feel as if I've stopped falling into a black hole and that I have landed alive in Margaritaville.

Hell, whatever scars I might have are only causes of celebration—that I've made it to the present, this now which is as naked as we are.

Pablo asks me where the North Star is but what do I know of space, of cosmic forms?

I kiss him slowly and he rubs his face against me.

I don't care if we are ghosts among ruins.

Right now, we're dreaming without even having to close our eyes.

"What will happen to us in the morning?" I stutter.

"That's a million years away," he whispers.

"But in the morning?"

"We'll see."

I nod my head.

In daylight, one can trust one's eyes.

In the dark, the body knows the route to survival.

We have instincts that have developed within us after millions of years of living and dying on Earth.

I become cold and we go back to bed where earlier our shapes, or the ruins of them, have been etched out in the sheets.

Our desires are often explicit.

■ ■ ■

Over the next year, Pablo and I become friends and stop sleeping with each other.

I'm a little surprised one March night to see him waiting for me as I stagger home from *Little Jim*'s.

I'm alone, broke and tired of my clothes smelling like smoke.

I smell like a goddamn fireman; the bars are becoming more and more like the hearts of volcanoes.

The truth is that I spent most of the night hugging the jukebox.

I didn't really want sex.

I do right now.

Only, it's Pablo who is here and we are now just amigos.

Pablo is as gone as I am, but I sense he is here for a safe place from some internal storm.

Riders of the storm.

He loves my apartment because if you open up the balcony door you can smell Lake Michigan.

Not that you can see it!

My building is one of the last rental unit in the lake shore area of New Chinatown.

Daily, I see yuppies shopping for outrageously expensive condos right in this building.

Soon I will have to move out, replaced by a young banker, a pretty actor, a successful photographer, or a dedicated accountant.

"Hola, El Cid," I smile. "Come inside. If you want to be cold, I'll put some ice in your wine."

He follows me inside, holds me, takes a deep breath.

"What are you doing?" I ask gently.

He holds me even harder. "I want to never forget how you smell like. The nose is one way that a poor man takes his revenge on a rich man's garden."

"Sit down. You're drunk."

"Ricky, you've been smoking tonight? Trying to pick someone up? Why don't you take the bull by the horns instead. You know what I mean?"

Many glasses of wine later, we stop talking.

We grow sullen as we next finish off the leftover and frowning rum.

Maybe this is what I miss most about not having a lover anymore: two bodies in one space not having to say anything to each other.

Pablo is still young, too young to be this unhappy. "So why are you here tonight?"

He becomes animated, as if a spell has been broken.

"You know about Chino. I mean, you know he's dead. You went to his funeral. They never caught the guys who did it, you know."

I move over by him. "I know, honey. Chino's probably in heaven looking down on us right now. Jerking-off, I hope."

Pablo pushes me away. "Ricky, he tried awfully hard to go to hell."

We say nothing for the next ten minutes.

Chino stole Pablo from me even though Pablo was never mine; I didn't want him until he was unavailable.

My family asks about Pablo although they are afraid that if I find a companion then I will demand for them to treat us as a couple.

A couple of thugs.

A couple of what?

Pablo starts talking and I know it's going to be one of his monologues; I'm right but first, "Stop, let me piss first and get bigger glasses for the vodka."

He follows me into the bathroom. “Why do you always know the right thing to say to me?”

“Pablo, a man needs his privacy sometimes.”

“I’ve seen you at the Belmont Rocks doing God knows what. It was hard to tell from where I was but your butt. . . .”

I zip up.

Glasses, vodka, ice, radio tuned to a classical station.

It’s the *New World Symphony*; I’d laugh at the selection but Pablo might think I’m laughing at him.

He speaks slowly, deliberately. “It’s my anniversary. Chino has forgotten all about me. The dead are putas, no? We went out just a couple of months. Then he got killed. And today is the fifth month anniversary of our first date. Chino was something special. That’s why he got stolen from me. You liked him, I know you did because you didn’t make jokes around him. You listened to him. Everyone did. Not any more. Chino doesn’t have a tongue. He doesn’t have hands. He doesn’t have those beautiful legs. He doesn’t have a cock. He doesn’t have a neck I wanted to bite tonight like I was fucking Dracula or something.”

He cries so hard that he is no longer saying words and I hold him.

Pablo’s Chino was killed in a drive-by shooting.

He had been in the wrong place and in the wrong time.

Pablo’s Chino.

Will I never belong to anyone?

I don’t know what to say and end up making Pablo angry with these words, “Honey, you celebrate the sixth month, a year, 25 years. But the fifth month, well . . .”

“Ricky, we have five fingers on each hand. Five. You should know. You jerk-off enough. You should know that five is important. Five. Five.”

He paces the room like a trapped animal.

I open the balcony door. “Take a deep breath.”

Pablo almost says something, stops and takes a long look into my tired face.

He then takes that deep breath.

"Lake Michigan!" I prompt. "There are some things you just can't see even if they're there."

Pablo leans forward, throws his glass of vodka in my face.

Startled, I fall back. "What?"

"I want to lick it off."

He does and we end up kissing.

"Let's just sleep tonight, OK?"

Pablo nods.

"Sometimes, Ricky, I have sex with a guy just to sleep next to him. To breathe in the air he's just breathed out."

I push him towards the bedroom. "You're sick and that's why you are the most perfect friend in the world for me."

"I think I'm going to be sick in the morning."

"If you're human," I add.

He whispers in my ear, "I love you, Ricky Ricardo Jr."

"I wish you did."

I put Pablo to bed and he floats away to some safe place in his head.

Why do I always feel like I'm being left behind?

Again.

Again.

Again.

My body is my true family.

My soul is the orphan that I've adopted.

My mother and father are sleeping in each other's arms and why can't I as a gay man have the same refuge?

Is my Uncle Linda going to make his cameo in a séance soon?

Again, I'm alone.

I am no loner and is that my tragedy?

Shakespeare is doing the cha cha cha in Chicago tonight.

I can't sleep.

I want to guard my friend against some invisible enemy tonight.

I sit on the couch, listening to my neighbors argue about alternative music not being alternative since it's so mainstream now.

Stupid shits.

I shake off my blue mood by thinking of someone I slept with (Did he even have a name? Did he ever share that much of himself with me?) who stayed over on a night when these very neighbors were going for each other's throats.

My boyfriend (who hadn't been a boy in a very long time) cooed, "They sound like jazz musicians without instruments."

He didn't know what a poet he was.

I remember him listening to the arguing couple some more, cocking his head like a dog that is left alone very often.

"Just listen to them go up and down the scale, baby."

I remember that much of him.

I still appreciate that much of him.

Is love possible?

I don't remember orgasm with him, just that moment listening to the neighbors.

Curious how the body is an amnesiac.

Are we all men of the mancha, our erect lances against windmills?

I'm glad to laugh at myself.

I turn on the television and fall asleep watching, of all things, *It's a Wonderful Life*.

Pablo talks in his sleep.

He talks in Spanish.

Angels get wings on the television every time a bell rings.

Is it a wonderful life?

My blue midnight blows out the candles, one by one.

I end up in the dark, face down.

I spite the gods by dreaming about reality.

The Europe of Their Scars

Two tourists fish in Portugal, their secret wounds healing. Their love of one woman hurries them home (a hotel), but the river in which they whispered all day long follows them. Their woman is at church, mermaid among saints. Vicente and Carlos whisper in a bar without a jukebox. They look like lovers to their lover when she arrives, breathless with her love of God. She is each man's true love, but that matters little to her, as it shouldn't. Carlos and Vicente accept her ghost and the three of them sit in alcohol's silences. As the men stagger to their shared room, the river itself replaces the fish that the men imagine catching in their minds. They don't love their woman after all. Europe is full of women and the two friends have each other. For right now, that is enough. They drink all night in their sinking room and watch the sun rise over the Europe that must accommodate their desires, whatever they are. They make love to each other and it is a surprise, that despite the years of knowing each other, they are still each mysterious. In the morning, they shave at the same sink, but say nothing. Nuns and priests would understand such private vows.

■ ■ ■

Ten years later, Vicente writes a letter to the dozing moon. He sends it by smoke, and returns to the wreckage of his weekend. He spills cigarettes on the stairs. Sits on the floor in his briefs. And waits. Is he in Paris again, if only by spirit? Doesn't it matter at all to his dazed soul? He lets the phone ring because his messiah will not have a voice. Wants for a friend, anyone, to read Shelley aloud to him. His beard draws him to morning. That trip to Europe changed his life, or consumed it. And now? He signs the letter by spilling wine over his chest.

■ ■ ■

Ten years earlier, in Italy, the one fed by the silk route, Vicente and Carlos see a slow life that's not theirs. From the gondola, the world seems church dark. Arm in arm, they become tourists once again. The prosaic, under moonlight, proves malleable to the youth of the men's Venice. The coherent tides take them to a dawn without souvenirs. Exteriors of bedrooms shine with spilled wine. Masqueraded mysteries go *home*. Then noon, time for tuxedoes, formal ape hour in yet another occasion. They stop to look at the sea, but Vicente and Carlos know it's too cold to swim in it or to belong to it. It's time to go back to colder climates, back to unstoppable weddings. Carlos wants to kiss in a doorway but Vicente isn't sure that God created lust to tempt mankind. Love, insists Carlos, sends the blood from the head to the cock. He holds Vicente's compass but the two men remain lost. They enter the currents of other humans and arrive at a party wearing identical frowns.

■ ■ ■

Carlos is exhausted by Barcelona's well-dressed dead at the discos. They beg him for breath, any slow kiss he can offer them. Men and women circle him, each one with valid reasons for a season in Carlos's mouth. The church bells swing from left ear to right ear. The drunk matador lifts his shirt to prove he has no scars. Then it's Carlos's turn: the crowd hushes. What do they see? Like any other gentleman, he borrows a cigarette from the suicide next to him. Carlos blows rings that turn Earth into Saturn. He bows to the applause. The bar mirror is used to miracles. The party returns to its pose as a constellation wannabe. Spanish women offer comforts which is beyond Carlos's particular pain, but how beautiful they are in their casualness, cruelty. He loves them today; what day is it? Friends are off getting high, but Carlos is an audience member of the try-outs for the newest Eve. Where is Vicente?

■ ■ ■

In London, a naked painter gives Vicente a tour of his "mistakes." And they are many, a pile of canvases, a landslide of colors. Then the men sit under an olive tree to talk about destiny as a shrug. The naked painter. Vicente in his expensive pants. Later in the week, the novelist is a tourist if only to develop calluses on his camera eye. In the church, a dragon blows fire from the other side of stain glass veils. A young existentialist eyes Vicente, and they go off into the ruins of a good wine. Vicente feels the wings of the dragon rush him down an ashy path. This is a moment of an important decision. He did not come to Europe to become a bitter man. He makes love like a conquistador, a terrifying night of power.

■ ■ ■

Carlos drinks wine in Dante Plaza in Denmark, not named for a poet but a knuckle fighter with unusually big hands. The pigeons try to peck out the sun's eyes in a foolish attempt to make blindness normal. Vicente's papers scatter, find exile in a cloud; he is left wordless. Time to rent an airplane and handsome pilot to get a bird's eye view of view; but first more wine, blood of an unlived day. Vicente's novel has to be novel or else he has wasted these drunk nights with the moon. A violinist collapses in a chair at the two men's table and they nod at each other, strangers linked by the geography of individual pain. The violinist thinks they are lovers but Vicente and Carlos have been arguing. Each of them go home with someone else, and in the morning they laugh at their foolishness. They shave together after their guests leave. Then they become lovers, body and soul.

■ ■ ■

In a French cafe, an American bluesman wails for the heartsick in this sea blue night. The saxophone speaks all the languages of the light in the slow sky over the living. Vicente gets homesick for an America that doesn't exist. His cigarettes send smoke signals to God from whose corpse has sprung this Parisian primitivism. Carlos makes a mental note to stop thinking so much and to just enjoy the ruins of his present reality. The bluesman is sad about a lover that may or may not be real. An unshaved, unwashed and unhurried Vicente stares at this performing unbared soul in all of his true ugliness or at least as much as he can without going blind. Carlos wonders what it would be like to be happy with a woman, but the moment passes. Soon, he's gossiping with the drunk moon.

▪ ▪ ▪

French museums crowd the mind with the stolen relics of homo sapiens across time and space. The headless statues of young Greeks reject evolution for they are timeless, never changing, stuck in poses. It is difficult to imagine anyone's destiny being different than one's own. Carlos stays there long enough to be able to have a story or two for friends at home. He is asked to buy hashish, but Vicente isn't interested in blurring the world he is responsible for now because of his claim of words. Soon he is late for an appointment, skips it. Watches men watch him. They think Vicente is a spy, sexy but carnivorous. He wears the morning beard of the unpublished. The novelist looks around him and Europe is invisible; he could be anywhere. Where was his best friend, Carlos? Why did the world only exist when they were together? But the two friends had agreed to meet at Campagna Beach in three weeks and each separated to the Europe offered in their personalized condom ads. Vicente had his first wet dreams in dry years and they were odd, the way the ocean is when it tugs at your ankles. It is both an invitation and a trap.

▪ ▪ ▪

Three weeks later, they meet once again, only on the beach, swimming until it gets too cold to be naked. They wait for something, someone, anything to return them to life before passports. Being displaced is also about having too many new places from which to choose. Being in love is worse than not being in love. The friends stay on that beach as long as they can and then fly home with the extra weight of tears in their suitcases. As the two men lose contact with each other in an America of shouting pitchmen, they grow feverish in their quietness. Vicente never finishes his novel. Carlos grows to be nervous about being naked before anyone but God. Were they as handsome as they seem in surviving photographs taken in the Europe of their scars?

Cyber Conquistadores

E-mail:

Dear Santo, sí, you, dude, the Internet is like gay heaven minus the Sundays! You were right! Gracias, ese, for setting up my Pinta to explore new worlds. Didn't believe we'd still be friends when you moved to Houston. But here u are! We are. Wow, lots of links to studs and angels. Eye candy tastes better with J-Lo feeding the ears. What borders? Oh, yeah, my new name is LocoCowboy. Amigo, gotta go. Will send pix soon! In birthday suit?

■ ■ ■

BLOG:

The human body shouldn't be as new as it still is, generation after generation. In some amateur galleries, the men look startled by the camera's flash, that silver mine dangling in the air. And now I'm to be one of the seen, a revelation without address, a first name, crowned by the words: IM me ASAP. I'm hanging out, loose, on. In cyber space, I'm a rope bridge over an abstract chasm. Columbus, each man is a world.

■ ■ ■

E-mail:

Santo, Santo: crazy shit in the world. Changed my name. Tops thought I was into S & M. Wanting to whack me to whack off. Any nudies of Enrique Iglesias? Trying to date in cyberspace bedworld. Is "dating" a real world anymore? New name: NinePiratas. ZorroZero is already someone else's mask.

■ ■ ■

Spam:

Hi, I'm Jimmy and I'm lonely. Get a gold card and visit me on my private yacht. I'll show you my anchor and you show me yours.

▪ ▪ ▪

—IM from Ramundo of this Mundo

This attached hot photo is not of me, but fate is promiscuous. I'm not 6 feet, not hairy, not blessed with cheekbones. On the inside, I'm a Latin Lover with seed money to burn. Trust me and I will send my own skin through night airwaves. For now, this angel is an ambassador from my chaos. Look at his church bells. Maybe we'll pray together soon, someday.

▪ ▪ ▪

E-mail:

Santito, I answer the personals because why not believe in this world? Optimism isn't the word I'd choose when I feel horny. Good news on that test (and I don't mean school). Let's just say I'm running out of condoms. As if. Why are you so quiet these days, con cariño, LunaDancer.

▪ ▪ ▪

Chat Room: Str8menLook2

Trucker007:

I once crossed America in stolen pink panties. Not as a drag queen, sorry. I'm growing a beard, Adamic billboard.

Macho3lips:

Seeking a Cadillac in this junkyard.

2big4yrgood:

Husbands seem to hang out in antique shops.

LunaDancer:

Is it raining men where u live n die?

Jrsl532mp:

Gracias to that sailor sharing his cyber sea legs. Any other sluts from Atlantis?

CARLOS8APES

Love goatees. Let's jump off the Ark right now!

■ ■ ■

E-mail:

OK, Santo, I send you a link to new naked men, vatos posing for Latino artists. No, nothing about spying. Those are boring and who needs straight men to pollute his fantasies with their pretend innocence? I'm not jaded, amigo, just want a country of my own. I want to be president of Sodom & Gomorrah. Everyone is going to war. I think it is my duty as a citizen to strip as many soldiers as I can! Hijo, did I make you laugh? Your heartbreak is mine. I have to change names again—cyber stalkers. Ignore pictures of me naked under palm trees because I'm not wearing sun block and glow like an apple begging to be kidnapped to Eden. An impulse, these days, is similar to building a permanent statue in God's mind. Hey, have I ever seen u naked when u were sober? Love, Matador4U2. Luv new names.

■ ■ ■

Spam:

Penis enlargement without anyone knowing! Conquer the world overnight!

■ ■ ■

E-mail:

Santo, idiota, there are men in cyber space waiting for u 2. Was the hospital terrible? No tacos there, I'm sure. Checking on flights. May have to make three layovers (not the fun kind). Flesh comes with problems, after you get dressed. Oh, I'm going to kidnap you to a clothing optional version of the Caribbean. Let's just say the skeleton key below your belt will open Kingdom Come. Smiling yet? I'm typing this on my laptop—isn't laptop just poetry? Now I feel your smile. I'll post where we are going to stay and play and bay in case any natives want to seduce us. Santo, trust me without one good reason to do so. This is the most writing I've done since starting that porno novel. No, it wasn't fun after the first three pages. So he left you. That makes it easier for you finally to be found. Idiota, pero mio, SkySwimmer69. SIDA isn't a death sentence anymore.

▪▪▪

Pedro, Webmaster:

I offer Gothic romances without romances. This embassy proves that sin still exists. Was Havana ever Havana? To be webmaster is to turn refuge into an art. These go-go boys go nowhere, and pleasure is proof that history isn't everything. Click here for thumbnails offered like diamonds in a pawn shop.

▪▪▪

Submission to Ezine, Assurances:

Hey, chulos, here are some poems for u. About luv & death. God doesn't have the copyright on everything. Poems are attachments, as yr guidelines say. Only have naked pictures of me. Digital. Of course I can get other pix. Guess could scam friends and scan myself. Hear from u soon?

▪▪▪

E-mail response to DallasDiego00:

I don't believe you're the devil. Not hung enough, not in your hand-held camera's stare. What do you mean u know what sites i go to? there is evil in the universe & cyberspace is part of the whole. but a tattoo doesn't make u god's rival. who isn't pierced these days. grow up, and don't e-mail me again. Or else.

▪▪▪

Homepage Visitor's Comments:

—Hey, dude, gracias for giving el pueblo a place in which to take off yr clothes so it gets easier to breathe

—I'm ashamed you have Latin blood in u. Do you know about Satan?

—Great bodies and for free! Poor but not poor in New Orleans.

—R u single?

—Please tell yr visitors about my site, Sailors: An Art Gallery

—Boring. All the dicks look the same. Needs drama. Do you know anything about the traditions of storytelling? A male body isn't inherently a story.

—Great, 2nd visit. Maybe more of yr poems?

■ ■ ■

E-mail sent to a ghost that bounces back:

Querido Santo, there is only your absence now. Ghosts should get mail privileges 2. I still think about us at the airport before u got stolen by sticky fingers in the sky: u scared at us having real bodies and me cruising pilots. Yr suitcase was like a raft in the middle of a hurricane. Can I blame God for luv as always? IM me, as in immediately. the dead should form a union and get some perks. hear me through all the noise of stars singing about their deaths light years ago? Santo, my Santo?

■ ■ ■

Welcome to my Paradise:

My homepage is dedicated to mi amigo, Santo. He is in Heaven for sure or else Satan does have a monopoly on the cosmos. I invite Santo to be the ghost in my machine, free rent. As you look at these men and links, try to imagine being young for an eternity. Hey, Santo, go AWOL once in awhile. I have lots of temptations here with your name written in magic marker on the men's naked chests.

■ ■ ■

E-mail:

Congratulations, this is an unofficial notice that you have been accepted into our MFA program. The reviewing committee found your work different and that is mighty close to original. You'll get a formal contract, letters, etc. I just want to add a personal aside: how can you be so young and be so scarred? You remind me of me.

■ ■ ■

Spam:

I'm a psychic and have the vibrations that someone you know isn't on this plane of existence. Credit cards accepted. Don't disappoint the dead by being cheap.

■ ■ ■

poem written 2 years later

Electric Feasts

As itchy as the *Old Testament*, I'm
the DJ's hostage, bouncing like a globe
turned basketball. I've promised amigos

to make contact with flesh and flash.
Sí, noise is an old god. It's good to have
a body—or does it have me? Swaying

like a scarecrow with only the wind as
a savior, I bump and grind to lure hombres
to envelope me with their hairy karma.

I love to misspend. The fog machine
tries to turn nowhere into NYC, all that
is left of babbling Babylon. I hate all this

and hurry home from the hurrah. I rush
back to my sweaty Web site where caught
questions linger like hard-ons taking

their gloves off. I tried the bars to get
away from my desk, but it *is* better here,
at this electric feast, at this porthole that

has such faith in semen, at this mirror
with moving parts. I click like a flamenco
dancer fucked up on unrepentant speed.

Conquistadores trade their nude shots
with me and we may form an army of lovers
that will lead a naked crusade to take back

our Sodom and Gomorrah. Until then, we
starve for each other, heartened to know
we're not alone in the unexplored

continents below our dreaming waists.
I click, type, take off my clothes and,
for a brief moment, the fig leaf is as

dated as the pony express, eunuchy,
or the missionary position. *I'm here*,
I write to the vast night, *what do you like*?

■ ■ ■

E-mail response to ElCidMan:

Google me: it's all i know about orgies lately. Sure i like my poems, but i wuld give it all up for 1 day with a lost amigo, not right another word. Free this weekend. How will i recognize u? i will be wearing my warrior spirit and tight jeans and carry a black notebook. in case an idea for a poem visits. i warn you that anything we do belongs to art.

■ ■ ■

A Thank You Ecard from ElCidMan:

It's of a naked conquistador with his sailors hooting and waving their brown arms and legs behind him. Underneath his feet are the words: *Thank you for being my treasure*.

Amateur Telenovelas

1. MIA

Arturo is drinking alone again. I can see him from my bedroom window that is next to his house even though he is acting as if he's not only condemned to be alone, but actually is by himself. I'm here watching him drink alone again. He sits in that exaggerated black chair the neighborhood calls "The Throne Not Even the Moon Wants." It's easy to find an excuse to leave my house, walk across the wet grass dressed in just my robe, not that he would care. Wrong. Not that I would care. Right.

I knock on one of his living room windows and he stares at me as if surprised that an owl has so many limbs, or that I'm the wrong lover on the wrong night. He stares at me. He stares at me, but not the way most men stare at a nearly naked woman appearing without an excuse knocking on his living room door while stars are dying over our heads. He doesn't even see me. He stares beyond me. There is something beyond me that my back knows better than my breasts ever will; of course, whatever it is isn't photogenic—philosophy often isn't. He is looking from some ship in search of a lighthouse, and upon failing to do so, continues its endless search rather than betray the royalty sponsoring the search for the nearest edge of the Earth where criminals can be effectively pushed off into unaccountable darkness.

"Mia?" I love his low voice. He opens the window and I lean forward. "Mia?" I drop my robe. "Arturo, I can see you from my bedroom window. One, I have a window. Two, I have eyes. Three, sorry. You are not invisible." He nods, pours me some wine. Arturo has never—ah, I almost said *allowed*—invited (we silly apes love cause and effect, no?) me into his house. What must the neighbors think of us drinking wine on opposite sides of an opened window, especially me in my Eve costume?

"Does it bother you that I'm naked?" I ask this knowing that he prefers men.

"As long as I'm not also naked with you." It's the warm answer that he would, of course, extend to me so that I don't feel embarrassed, even though my bare ass is just another ember in the moonlight. I nod; I know his dance; I know almost all of the dances that men with their three legs can dance. "I just wonder if I really am beautiful or maybe I'm just a prisoner of my ego?" I throw my head back so that he can see the tiniest hairs on my Adam's apple. I gulp down his sweet red wine; please, I don't want to sound like a bee in love with the idea of honey when it's honey I need.

A cold wind passes through the night, but not even it can push me into Arturo's arms; the leap is mine to take. I ask for more wine and as he leans forward to pour I pretend to pull ice cubes out of my breasts.

Arturo shrugs, "What's an abstract artist like me got to do with anything as real as you?"

"I know about the men that sleep here." Arturo swallows his wine; some vices, I think, are rather biological. I'm suddenly afraid that he is going to storm out of his living room and so I throw my body towards him the way a mermaid—one caught between sea and land—might really mean to do as she abandons her genes for a dream lover. No, I don't understand Arturo.

He kisses me on the cheek and whispers in my ear. "Men stay at your house all night. Here, my men tend to evaporate, as if I just dreamt them up."

It's neither an insult nor a compliment. So Arturo has noticed me and my activities across the long lawn where my life is anything but a matter of choice, choices. Life, what a beautiful choice. I didn't even choose to be born. It's true that I have had many lovers and can and will have many more. They've offered me everything, but I've come to realize that I want more than anything that is a thing. For example, I want to be left alone. Being alone is not a thing. Arturo will leave me so alone that I will have to hunt him up to remember why I hate him. I don't hesitate: "Arturo, I must marry you."

He eyes me. I have his curiosity—not a bad start for a relationship. He looks at me as if I'm a spinning top that will give pleasure to the observer when it stops, flops over, grows dead still. Arturo kisses me on the forehead and I don't know how to kiss him back. "You don't want me," he laughs so that the breath from his mouth stokes the stars so they won't die, not tonight. "You don't want me, Mia because I'm good for nothing and you and I have nothing in common—we only have that, darling."

I step back, grab my robe, run toward my house, stop and turn around. I open my arms and wear the wind like some coronation gown. Why do the poor never lose their dreams? Fuck it; I'm so tired of feeling this optimistic but I am bursting with such unused energy. Me and Arturo. He is busy drawing his curtains—as if they're real walls. I slip into my bed. I will sleep. I need all the energy I can steal from the universe to institute my plan.

2. MIA'S FATHER

Imagine a man at my age having to fight for his daughter's honor when he isn't even sure she is even his daughter; I'm sure there is no such thing as honor either for the living or for the dead. Screw the sex of the offended or the offender. Still, to come home to three men in my daughter's bedroom is too much, even for an atheist like me, an ancient atheist. I throw punches and Mia's young men who have worked for me in my garage over the years, respect me too much to either hit me back to disappear down the street while laughing out of their asses like I'm just a chili bean dispenser. I'm more than that: I'm less, true, than what I wanted to be. When you're from the Midwest, you're not from the East or the West—not Hollywood, not New York. My wife is screaming and screaming. I haven't released myself from even my own dreams of my cock being a palm tree withstanding a hurricane so ancient that it has no name. She is screaming at Mia and her three men. Oh yes, I must protect what isn't ever going to be my issue. Mia is quiet. I speak with my gray fists. Goddammit, I feel old. I am old.

But still my daughter and the three men who are taking advantage of her is enough for me to throw punches. I punch hard. It's actually quite wonderful when the four of us—four men—become entangled in each other's bodies. Like any respectable tumbleweed in any John Wayne movie, we roll into the streets where my neighbors jump into the mess because their lives are publicly less messy. Ernesto, Mia's latest boyfriend—her last, as far as I'm concerned—is suddenly naked, so I take off my shirt, give it to him. He takes the shirt; by throwing it around the little he has, that act makes us practically related. He smiles at me and I throw my most impolite punches. Each ugh, each ooh, each thump drives every one in the crazy mob mad for we all want blood as a taste, as a mask. Blood. The three men I found in Mia's bed with Mia are on the other side of my neighbors who want to beat me up for their own reasons and so I try to kill them too. I can't even kill God in private. The three boys—when did they become handsome men I would be proud to call my own sons?—throw their arms around each other and limp away from the riot. Oh my God, it's a riot without personal invitations. "Mia," I'm screaming. "Mia." "Mia." "Mia." "Mia, get out." "Mia, you have no house." "Mia, you have no fucking father or mother." I can't stop myself. I do try to stop. Stop. Please stop me, God, or Mia will never be my daughter again. Please, God, please. I can't stop. "Mia, you whore." "Mia, I curse you for being as beautiful as your mother and you are as big a curse as she has been all my days and most of my nights." All of this is in front of neighbors who have stopped punching each other in each other's crotches; no, I will give birth to this day because it wants to give birth to me and I won't allow it. Arturo is grabbing me, but I'm not chasing spirits. I won't let my ass be kicked by Mia's boyfriends who can barely grow a goatee. That really means something, something. Arturo is determined to stop me from fighting. He isn't even a policemen. Arturo, a painter of naked men. Arturo, naked before his male models in their model behaviors. Arturo is the one stopping me from kicking the shit out of some worthless bastard, a neighbor who stole the color I was about to paint my house once. Who isn't a freak in this sideshow? This thought gives me scary energy. I pound Arturo where I can only imagine that he is hiding his crotch. Pound. More weight. Evil neighbor. Evil neighbor. He is stronger than I am and kicks me in the ass. When I fall face-first into the mud, he sits on my head. I thought Death was, at the very least, heterosexual. I don't die. I may never die. Mia grabs his hand, and I sit up. I watch them. Mia wants him. He doesn't want Mia. I roll on the ground. My wife runs to me. Mia has a suitcase in her hands; she's set this all up. I admire the bitch. Why do I call my own daughter a bitch? Like I don't have enough shame; maybe I don't; Mia and Arturo walk arm and arm until she's swallowed up inside his house; my wife slaps me because she, like me, doesn't know what else to do. We do what we can with our bodies. I slap her back. Mia is inside Arturo's house. Mia may be living inside Arturo's house. How many times I've called the police because I've seen naked men inside of there. What the fuck do I care that he was painting them; like fucking art should exist in my neighborhood. Mia, my Mia, walked in there, with a suitcase filled with clothes I bought for her before I knew she loved making love as much as I do but her mother doesn't. Mia, mine. I once climbed my apple tree just to see Arturo paint a naked man. He is a moral danger to the greater collective of we who have agreed to pretend we will pay off our mortgages before we're dead. The lights in Arturo's house go off. Mia, Mia, Mia. Arturo walks out and offers me his hand. He can't offer me his cock, because I know what I know. Yeah. Mia, Mia, Mia. Arturo said in a shaky voice, "Fine." "What the hell do you mean by fine? Fine is a last name, a fine art. Fine?" My wife knows her cue and grabs my arms so I won't punch out Arturo. How I love her at that moment and I try to remember the first time I raised her skirts, the first time she opened up her legs to me, the first time we rowed into a foggy morning which might be tomorrow which, of course, isn't Arturo's business. Mia, Mia, Mia. Arturo spits into my ears: "Fine, I'm going to marry her. You win." Mia, Mia, Mia. "You hear me old man. I'm marrying Mia. She lives with me starting tonight. She decided that." I feel my hand go limp inside Arturo's version of a wedding night handshake. He lays me on my back. I want to kiss Orion. No, he is a man. He was a man. Mia and Arturo? Arturo bows to the neighbors who unceremoniously mock his ass—hey, this is my backyard and I'm not looking for a scarecrow, assholes—neighbors who can't wait to fault either my wife or me for our daughter, the most beautiful woman in our neighborhood now pretending to join Arturo in his artistic bed. He leaves me, and walks into his house. All the lights in his house go off. Light after light my daughter becomes an orphan. Leave me one light, I pray, so I can make a wish by it. It, something in the universe. Mia, Mia, Mia. Mia shuts Arturo's living room window, the one that faces us and God. The neighbors, tired of fighting, start to shriek in high voices I never heard at any bar-be-cue. I go into the backyard and pick up an axe. My wife is screaming again. Estrogen, curse Satan, isn't a goddess yet. I will kill Arturo, but not tonight. I stare into his house and calm down knowing there is just one gay man with my daughter, instead of three men who not only desire her but whom she might desire in return. My neighbors follow me into my backyard. It's awfully dark. I thrust the axe, with all the strength I have come to claim as mine, into the apple tree that is proving to be the tree of everything but good or evil. Stroke. Stroke. Stroke. It will take time for me to destroy this tree, but what else does an old man like me have to do but defy Time? Stroke. My wife stops me, whispers: "At least we'll have a son-in-law who can afford to give us—both of us, love—decent funerals," Stroke. She is right. Stroke. Arturo's house is dark. Mia is sleeping somewhere in Arturo's house. Stroke. I can't stop myself. I chop away. I chop away. Stroke. Baby, come home. I did my best to give you a home. Stroke. Arturo, she's my baby. I chop away. My wife never sleeps without me within her arms. I chop away. She walks to me and asks me to forgive Mia. No. But I forgive her my wife, my bride, my lover. I forgive her for loving me.

3. MIA'S MOTHER

"At least we have a son-in-law who can afford to give us decent funerals," I say this yet one more time, but Ernesto doesn't hear it again. This is my new rosary prayer. "At least we have a son-in-law who can afford to give us decent funerals," I say yet one more time.

Ernesto ignores me. Finally, he clears his throat. "I was planning to marry Mia, with or without you or her father's permission."

"Ah," I laugh over my coffee cup, "but was she planning to marry you?"

Ernesto knows this is the kind of question that cannot be truly answered, but something inside him wants to give voice, to give shape, to give away an uneasiness deep within him. "You're Mia's mother. Does she ask after me?"

"She lives next door. That's a country I'll never see with my own eyes. My husband says Mia is dead so Mia is dead even though I see her with my own eyes. These eyes are mine. That's for sure. I have ears too. I hear gossip. About their wedding. About their sleeping arrangements. All this gossip is like pictures on a postcard. They're not the real country. Just a postcard. Once I got a postcard with a picture of a bunch of French pastries that I would never taste. Not even if I was a witch. Even if I gave Satan himself a ride on my ass to the moon and back. Do you understand me, Ernesto?"

He pounds his fist against the counter. "It's my fault. I never thought I was growing up."

I nod my head. "Her father was especially angry that you were in that mess. He loved you like a son. It was like incest. It was and it wasn't."

He shrugs, walks over to the kitchen window for sign of movement in Arturo's house.

For some unknown reason, I keep it a secret that Arturo and Mia, as I spy on them during their daily schedules, are at the beach. Arturo paints and Mia is painted. "Unpredictable," I say aloud.

Ernesto gives me a strange look. "What do you mean?"

"Ah, that she married Arturo. You might as well as forget her." I pour him some more coffee. I wonder if it's the caffeine or his anger that makes him shake so. Ernesto's body fills up the kitchen with the smell of maleness that no amount of coffee can quite mask. I'm filled with a surprising pride that this young man aches so much for someone or something. I knew a wisdom like that deep inside me, so long ago.

"I need more sugar," he says in a depressed voice. I pour spoon after spoon of white. I pretend that Ernesto and I are lovers, and that I'm refueling his body with spoonfuls of white sweetness that I took from him all last night. I can't stop myself from laughing. Ernesto puts his hand over the coffee cup, but I can't stop myself from pouring one last spoon of sugar. I pour it over his hand. It's my way of saying goodbye.

4. ERNESTO

This is my chance! I push myself through the opened living room window and fall into a heap at Mia's feet. She doesn't act startled. Maybe that's a good sign. I look up at her, and she is so far away from me.

"I miss you too, Ernesto," she finally sighs.

I take a deep breath. "I miss you too, Mia."

"So it seems. Wine?" I nod. "Is he home?"

"He?"

I nod, "Arturo."

"My husband. I thought you hate wine?"

I spot a bottle of vodka and hold onto it as if it's a life preserver. "Mia, it's over. Leave with me. Now. You and me and this bottle of vodka. Or take a bottle of wine if you want. We can toast each other. In my bed."

Mia isn't wearing a wedding ring. A wave of confidence breaks against my skull and heart. She walks up to me and holds me like she used to, as if she was climbing down the tree of the knowledge of good and evil in the Garden of Eden. She is Juliet ready to elope. Mia whispers in my ear. "Ernesto, I'm so happy these days."

"With him?" I hold her tighter and tighter.

"With myself. I'm no one's daughter. No one's girlfriend."

I won't let her escape my embrace. "And no one's wife?"

She kisses my eyelids shut. "I made him marry me. Imagine that."

I'm hit on the chin with this news. "He'd rather fuck me than fuck you." She tries to push me away, but I can't let her go. No, to be honest, I won't let her go. I mustn't let her go. Something in me—maybe some ancestor was a python—wants to crush her until she is as flat as photograph I can slip into my wallet. "If you're pregnant, I know it's mine. I did you first. Before those other guys. It's my baby. Mia, marry me."

She is too smart for me. Instead of fighting me, Mia embraces me back until something in me thaws. My arms and legs let her go. They open up the way a plant yields to sunlight after a stormy night.

Arturo's voice booms from behind me, "Son?"

I'm afraid to turn around. My body twitches from the anticipation of gunfire, bullets passing through me. I pray to St. Sebastian, the first holy man full of holes.

"Arturo," I say in a low voice, turning around slowly. He has no gun. Arturo doesn't even have a shocked look on his face. He takes the bottle of vodka away from me. I look at Mia, and she is also frightened. *Mia is alive! She is afraid of something. But why Arturo?* I half-expect him to break the bottle over my head. Instead, he grabs a glass, pours a double in it and offers it to me. I'm compelled to accept it. Mia walks to his side and kisses the open palm of his right hand. What should I do? What should I do? What should I do?

Mia interrupts my thoughts, "Arturo, this boy says he loves me and that I should leave you."

Arturo smiles at some other idea he doesn't share with either Mia or me. He says slowly, "I bet he doesn't even have enough money for a taxi. The taxi's on me. The rest, my good man, is yours to figure out. Bye, Mia." He leans over and kisses her on the right cheek. What game is this?

Mia's face becomes a stranger's mask. She eyes me up and down and tilts her head at Arturo, "When I can pay for my own taxi, then I'll go. I'll be the one kissing both of you goodbye."

I have to get out of here. Arturo stops me, "Ernesto, another one?"

Without an answer he pours me another double. I notice he has some wine himself. When did Mia become this sober? After her honeymoon night with Arturo? He motions for me to sit and as I do, they sit arm in arm in the sofa. "Darling Mia, what will the neighbors think of us entertaining at this late hour?"

She banters back, "Father thinks you're going to pay for his funeral so he isn't in any special rush to die. I think he's . . . puzzled." Maybe the old Mia does exist under these new clothes, this new attitude. I don't like being dismissed.

"Arturo, give me your right hand. Please. Sir?" My even voice startles them. I stand up. "I know what I know," I say gently. That I can still surprise Mia fills me with joy. I don't care about Arturo. Mia's face is a sign that maybe I still have a chance with her, that she isn't yet embedded in this life. Arturo gives Mia his glass of wine and opens up his right hand. "Palm up," I smile. He does it. I unzip my pants. The honeymooners are both frozen. Perfect. I take out my penis and testicles and place them in Arturo's hand, as if he is the keeper of some cosmic scale. "You can paint me Arturo. I'll pose nude for you." Arturo tries to pull his hand away but I don't let him. Mia is fascinated. I've gained something tonight. My desperation is a talent I must develop. I say, with a break in my voice, "This way you both get the man you really want." I look Arturo in the eyes. I let him go, zip up. I pour myself a new drink. Mia runs out of the room into dark spaces that I will someday map and name after my own desires and destiny. Arturo pours himself some vodka. Romanticism can only help you so much. He sits in the black chair and looks at me for something to say. It's time for me to go. I don't know what to say to Arturo. He has never hurt me and I've wounded him in some way. I thought my body was enough of a sacrifice. I say nothing. I don't want to use the door. I crawl out of the very living room window through which I entered. Maybe I can break the chain of events my entry has started. Once Pandora's box is opened, it'll never grow a new hymen again. I learned about this at the Church's sex education classes. I'm on solid ground, look up at the stars. Arturo leans through the window, "Tomorrow. The beach. Noon."

I say nothing for nothing tastes so sweet on my tongue and inside my head. There is a living river inside me and no one can tell that I am drowning inside it. I'm afraid of whistling in the dark for I will not be responsible for shattering the moon. I pass Mia's parents' house and it's as dark as my armpit hair. I'm afraid. Am I the only living thing in the world tonight? Wait, the man-on-the-moon! We dance with each other until I'm home. Taking off my clothes, it is a little startling to have proof that I am no ghost. The victorious have very little need for dreams. I will wear tomorrow's sunrise like a crown.

5. SYLVIA, ERNESTO'S TWIN

"So, my baby brother actually remembers me," I say with just the right amount of malice. Ernesto looks drunk, but it's too early in the afternoon for that. Drugs? He's too poor for any vice but sex. He doesn't smell of a woman. Or a man. It's strange being a fraternal twin because Ernesto and I are ultimately just linked by the day of our births. I'm nothing like him and for that I thank God, Satan, Buddha, Karl Marx, Eva Perón, Madonna and Robert Burns. I always hedge all my bets.

"It's you who can't forget me," he finally answers after several gulps of coffee. "Take off your sunglasses. You don't look evil. Just stupid."

People in the *Stone Porpoise* have seen us here so many times that we're ignored. Sometimes when Ernesto is drunk he becomes popular because he'll buy any stranger a drink. The regulars know that he's not wobbly yet. They wait. I buy the bartender a double and so we get our drinks for free. Ernesto is growing a goatee and I like it on him. It turns him into some English fop. He smiles at my compliment. "I need my sister to call me a goat. Keeps me humble. What's going on with you?"

Can I really tell him what is going on or is he being rhetorical again? I'm a court recorder and increasingly I'm getting better and better at substituting the words of witnesses for words from my own imagination. At first, I took guarded chances and changed a word like "wife" for "knife." Take that stake in your heart, Freud. I joined in the laughter with the judge over my early "mistakes." I learned to substitute entire sentences and not words. The bigger one thinks, the less likely the small-minded reader will dare challenge you. I have the fantasy of taking notes during an entire trial while actually writing a romance novel about a pirate from the Canary Islands. A substituted sentence here or there doesn't a romance novelist make. Not yet.

Ernesto and I sit in a familiar silence. It is the silence we so often shared on the rooftop of our childhood home. Up there, we'd pull apart the legs of an ant, the petals of a daisy, the tapestry of our parents' nightly arguments that inevitably unraveled, word by word, inspired us to look at the blind stars and gain a tremendous and important sadness knowing that light was as vulnerable as we were to forces inside its own true nature. I vowed, then, to never be powerless. Ernesto wondered if the man-on-the-moon was a peeping tom. His body changed long before mine did and he came to believe that his crotch was holy, at first. Eventually, it has become an unholy anchor or a poor octopus dreaming of wings.

He's done his duty to his older sister by minutes and is ready to go. I grab him by his right arm. He smiles at me but says nothing because he knows that I will fill up the silence with something important. "Ernesto, I know you pose naked for Arturo at the beach.

Mia on your lap. It might even make us a tourist site here. I don't care. That's not why I asked you to meet me here."

He leans forward and combs my eyebrows. It's our secret signal. Ernesto is really here! "I think I killed someone."

"Sylvia?"

"I'm not sure." He takes peppermint candy out of his leather coat pocket and offers it to me. It looks like a flower bud. "Who did you kill?"

"God."

He is angry with this answer. "You just want to know if I'm fucking or getting fucked. You're like the rest of them." He pulls away from me and I'm lost.

"Ernesto, wait."

"I didn't kill God. It's worse than that." He turns around. The bar grows silent. God, Ernesto is handsome.

"I killed Satan. Maybe God too. I killed them by not believing in them."

A woman overhears me, laughs until she literally shakes the bar. Ernesto puts on his sunglasses, gives me a salute and walks into the sunlight. The bartender seats me down. He buys me a drink. Many drinks. I won't sleep with him because Satan is dead. I sleep at home, wearing moonlight for a pair of pajamas. I jump out of the plane. I'm naked. The wind feels different in my crotch hair than in my ear hair. The earth grows larger even as I refuse to shrink before it, my birthplace. Even the air in my lungs feels heavy, a burden. Rocky the Flying Squirrel floats by like any other oak tree leaf from Maine, USA. My left arm wants to declare independence from my right arm but my sternum has a very unpopular opinion: let's remain one. I try to throw the weight of my brain into the heels of my feet and that causes me to make zero gravity in the air with my body. It used to be my body. I try to erase the mathematics of the perfect four directions that my arms and legs are in love with. A tree enlarges into a plot that becomes an island which comes to peter out into just a continent, which on historical cue, is slowly fleeing from other continents. The sea is a poor trampoline. I wake up in a world monopolized by God.

Father Fortunado will do his best and failing that, he will understand my fears. I've never met a man or woman more afraid of everything in my life. He is my role model. Sometimes I wear his dresses and we play the Great Gatsby game—what is of this world remains in this world. Sometimes I get to be Daisy although I'm never patient enough to wait around to be plucked.

6. FATHER FORTUNADO

Someone knocks on my door. "It's me, Sylvia."

"Por favor, not tonight."

"Father Fortunado, I did something awful."

"Just remember the word 'awe' in 'awful'." Silence.

"Just one moment, please?" she pleads.

"No, tomorrow." I hear her move away, move into the streets, and then suddenly she is no more real than the wind that finds me naked in my bed.

I feel as if I might suddenly turn into a giant. I'm God's Hulk. But I'm literate. Between my legs, there is a pad of paper and a pen. I push my humanness out of the way and write this:

ST. GABRIEL LALEMENT, MARTYR.
When the burning embers were pushed into my eyes, I lost my faith and regained my body. I twisted, arched as if giving birth to myself. The Iroquois grew tired of hitting me, and although I wanted to be a good guest, I couldn't die. No, I didn't want to, my body parts reintroducing themselves with each blow. When that tomahawk smashed my skull, I had no ideas left but strangely enough I was dancing. My body touched the four directions until I was no longer a man, but a world. Although blind, I saw the darkness push into me like a river where the baptized and unbaptized stripped and sang. Then nothing. Finally.

Not bad.

Not bad at all.

Finally—what a beautiful word.

There must be a God or else how else would we have garlic?

I've forgiven so many in the name of everyone but me.

I think it's a shame that evolution is taking away our fur, one hair at a time.

So it's not noticeable?

The gun looks like a theater begging for an audience.

I am not God's mistress, no matter how many Popes there have been.

An investigation, they said.

A witch hunt, I said.

Language really has the power to shape the universe.

The gun wants to sleep without ever dreaming again.

No, that's me.

The gun is a gun is a gun.

Don't think of it as a deposition, but more like a confession. Easy for them to say that.

As if the world needs more apocrypha.

I then pull the trigger and my head bursts, turning into a rose grown on Mars, the reddest of planets in the limited universe we know.

7. SYLVIA

I have to do something in the wake of Father Fortunado's suicide. I cut out the newspaper stories. Most of them avoid the grimmest details, but details are what make up the seconds that make up the minutes that make up the hours, that make up Eternity. For example, if I don't respond to the name of Sylvia, then I'm just a woman. I'm a pregnant woman. In two months, my breasts will be tuned by selfish tiny hands like some midget turning my nipples, like knobs on a radio that can be searched for favorite dance music. Another detail: mail addressed to Sylvia. It's a letter from Father Fortunado. *Tell my son goodbye and to think of me every time he looks into the marks in his palms.* It'll be a daughter. Of course it will. I told Father Fortunado that it would be a daughter but he only loved one woman. It wasn't me. It always was Mia. If I was a man, I might love Mia too. I take down the pictures of Father Fortunado I taped in the back of my bureau, so no one would see them. Here's one where he and I are sitting on the roof of the gymnasium. Who took this picture? Who would dare take this picture? My priest is dead while God still lives in some far away mansion or black hole. It doesn't seem fair, right. Kick, little girl, kick harder. Maybe you'll be a dancer. A spotlight is a spotlight and it's the one thing this town certainly doesn't have. My baby didn't push Father Fortunado over the edge. He was secretly very happy. To protect his name, I slept with as many men as I could find. Everyone thinks this baby is Alfredo's baby. I guess if you're a father once before, everyone assumes that lightning is going to hit the lightning pole one more time. They think I spent so much time with Father Fortunado because I had so many sins to confess. I did, but not through the mouths they thought! Alfredo was here, just earlier today. His fat face was quivering with sadness for me and for one moment I was touched and wondered what he might have looked like as a young courtier with flowers in his right hand and his left hand stuck in his pocket so I wouldn't notice the shaking.

Alfredo said, "I hear a new priest is coming in a week." I shrug.

Alfredo said, "Sylvia, we'll name the boy after Father Fortunado."

"It's going to be a girl. It has to be a girl."

Alfredo eyes me the way a horse looks at a mule, as if somehow we should be communicating but somehow unable to. "My wife has heard about you. Us."

"I told her myself. That this baby isn't yours. It's mine."

Tears well up in Alfredo's eyes. "No one has ever tried protecting me before. I'm touched."

I wipe his face with a dish towel. "Alfredo, go back to your old life. This baby is God's now."

"You mean you're giving it to the church orphanage, like Father Fortunado told you?"

Why are men so simple? My priest is dead. I'm not. The kicking in my stomach is all the philosophical proof I need to confirm that I'm right. "Alfredo, go home and never come back."

"Never?"

I turn my back and stare at myself in the mirror. It's true pregnant women glow. So do widowers. So do pregnant widows. A joy fills up my body. Sylvia is a survivor. Yes, this Sylvia, me. Father Fortunado has put his seed in me because he knew that I would own the future. We—the baby and me. Who would have ever guessed that I am stronger than God and Satan?

8. RAÚL, ERNESTO'S, AND SYLVIA'S LITTLE GROWN-UP BROTHER

I can't stand being in the house with Sylvia, my sister. I watch Alfredo go home and wonder if I can somehow pickpocket him without him catching me. This town is that boring. I put my arm around him, "Hey, how is my future brother-in-law?"

Alfredo pulls away, "You bastard, you won't get one penny of my fucking money. Now go get your asshole lubricated."

"Is that the kind of sweet talk you used on my sister? She said you had charm. Does that make her a snake charmer?"

I put my left arm around his waist and whisper into his ear, "I gotta tell you what my parents are saying. It's important, friend."

He doesn't want to trust me, but suddenly he slows down and walks like the old man he finally and truly is. I pull him closer to me. "No one must hear."

He stops in the middle of the street.

"Are you crazy? People will wonder what we're doing," I say, pulling him ahead. He follows and I lower my arm that much more.

"My father says he is going to kill you so you better buy him a gift. It's bad luck to die in a week when the town has no priest."

He agrees. I put my hand into his ass pocket. Alfredo doesn't notice because he is occupied with the exhilarating adrenaline that comes along with any melodrama. "Raúl, do you think your father would like a new television?"

I need more time. "No, you know him, he's always outside."

"True, true. How about something for fishing? But he has everything, doesn't he?"

I pull the wallet out slowly.

Alfredo asks me, "If I brought him the best Cuban rum in town, would he think this a present or would he mistake it for a sign that I'm divorcing my wife to marry Sylvia? That's out of the question. My wife, well, she's that."

The wallet is in my hand, and I'm suddenly bored. I bump into Alfredo. I bend down and pretend to pick up the wallet from the road. "Hey, look what you almost lost."

He gives me the eye of a store detective who has followed the wrong twin. He grabs his wallet and walks away. What the hell? I go to the beach. Arturo and his harem are painting and being painted. He has posed Mia and Ernesto, naked in a bed of seaweed. I once slept with a sailor because he lost a bet to me. He thrust his hips into me, and I kept yelling, come on, tear me apart with your blue body. It turned him on. Come on Roman slave, my asshole is an escape tunnel. Dig it out. The not-so-strange stranger held on to my shoulders like a charioteer. I was giving him a ride out of town. Is that all you have? He was touching something inside me that wasn't either Lust or Love. It wasn't Pleasure. He pushed my head into the pillow, sticking my ass up. He wasn't going to come. So that was his plan. If he didn't come, then it was only about me. I rocked him like the sea itself. His oar was taken further and further from any familiar shore. He got disoriented. The man who was just a boy a few years older than me arched back, and released the way a drowning man has no choice but to let go of that last breath. No matter the cost. I didn't come. He punched me in the eye. He jumped into his clothes and ran out. The throbbing in my eye was similar to the throbbing in my asshole. I want to love. I will love someday.

Mia sees me and waves at me and so I'm forced to wave back. Ernesto puts his right hand over his right eye as if either giving me a salute or trying to figure out who's there that his beloved Mia greets so familiarly. Tu hermanito! That Mia is not only beautiful, but also brilliant. We have so much in common the way we have to use our bodies in order to escape our dull fates so we can concentrate on our spiritual selves.

I lie down on the beach, pretending to wait for some phantom ship.

Arturo walks up to me and I look up into his crotch. It's the only game I know I can win. "Raúl, if you're going to come here everyday and watch me watch Mia and Ernesto as I paint them, then get busy."

He drops a package at my feet and walks away, back to his canvas. Mia and Ernesto laugh at me and I'm a little jealous of the new joy in their affections toward each other. I undo the brown package. It's almost as big as I am. It's a canvas, paints, and brushes. "What the fuck is going on?" I yell across the sand, hoping to sound brave at the exact time I feel scared.

Arturo yells back, without taking his eyes of his canvas. "As long as you're always here, paint me paint Mia and Ernesto. Bring that first painting to the house when it's done."

"I can't paint." Not in public. Being an artist in our town is a neon sign saying: last faggot for 69 miles. I mean, saying it aloud. It means you're a one-man plague of mariposas. Even as I say all this to him, I'm tearing at the plastic covering around the paints. "I need 365 more canvases. It's the Year of the True Brush."

They don't respond because they're already busy in their own projects. I open up a jar of red paint. I lean the canvas against a protruding boulder because I don't have a tripod and dip the brush into the liquid fire. Instead of two naked people, I see a series of roses whose petals leave a trail in the sunlight. How to capture that? I'm jealous that Arturo has such confidence in materiality, while I can't even control my own body. It's getting to the point that when I masturbate, body parts are less important than the story I put them into: like when I'm being kidnapped on Columbus's Santa María, or when I'm the towel boy in a submarine, or I'm lost in a Greek statue garden where the Beast is bored with Beauty and seeks GM born under Scorpio's bed of stars, non-smoker, flexible in past life fantasies. Each nude holds fruit and starfish, and soon they are a species which might evolve into the arch enemies of all of God's angels. I paint a cross instead of Ernesto's crotch, out of respect for my big brother. Mia gives birth to a hurricane. Green floods the canvas. Birds fly too quickly to trap them into the cage of my canvas. Arturo walks over to see what I'm doing. He looks. I look at him looking. He says nothing and returns to his canvas. He looks at it. Arturo walks over to Ernesto and Mia and they look at my direction. I'm dipping into Babylonian Blue. I mustn't hesitate, I tell myself. They get dressed. Arturo packs up. Ernesto and Mia run ahead. Arturo opens up his arms, as if I'm to join them, but I can't. I'm not done yet and I don't need models; they're actually obstacles. God's grace is a gesture of yellow in a paint that's not mine. I throw sand into the canvas. Some of it sticks. Some of it is too thick for light to pass through it. I look up. Everyone but me is gone from the scene of whatever crime I have committed. I take off my clothes and swim into the sea. My painting won't go away. I keep diving, again and again. It's so salty down there that I have to close my eyes. I close my eyes, but upon opening them again, the world hasn't changed. The canvas is still there, against a boulder. Arturo, Mia and Ernesto are still gone. I step out of the sea and my sex seems so small that I wonder how it has come to define my life and the lives of so many other humans around me. My clothes taste sweet. I'm tempted to throw the canvas into the sea, as if it's what Neptune exactly needs for his coral-tiled living room. I take it with me. Maybe I'll give it to Sylvia's baby. I'm going to be an uncle long before I establish my own relationships. This is unnerving. I pass the *Stone Porpoise* and I'm tempted to enter. But not with this painting shit on me. I pass Alfredo's house and all the lights are turned on. Arturo's house is dark. If I wasn't religious, I'd be afraid of vampires tonight. I pass the church where poor old Father Fortunado's ghost must be condemned to give guided tours to the believing. *If a priest can be so overwhelmed by sins, some of them his, then what hope is for us who war against the idea of death?* I'm tired, but when I see Sylvia headed toward me I try to act like I'm stronger than our father. She is puzzled by what I carry. She is going to the *Stone Porpoise*, but not to drink: just to smell wine, beer, vodka, whiskey and piss into a night that never needs to be cleaned and dressed for success.

"Sylvia, I can't join you. I'm busy tonight. I'll see you tomorrow."

She kisses me on the cheek and I'm unnerved when she says, "So you think there is really such a thing as *tomorrow*?"

9. ARTURO

I'm busy looking for something on TV, but there are only repeats of telenovelas. They're like the Bible if written by anti-intellectuals. There's a knock on my door.

"Ah, Raúl. Come in, come in."

"I brought you a present."

"I'm running out of walls. This house isn't prepared to be a museum dedicated to you."

He walks around and notices what no one else would—paintings have been rearranged in the house.

"They left together? The bastard didn't even tell me."

I motion for Raúl to sit down. "I gave them wedding money enough to start up in a bigger city. They'll invite us to their housewarming."

"Ernesto needs to be here. For Sylvia."

"You mean for you and for me."

He nods and I pour us a quite subtle wine smuggled out of the industrial vineyards of Southern California. It burns nicely.

"You need to go to art school."

"It's too late to seduce me like that."

"You have talent."

"Face down?"

I am nervous, like the first time I wore a man's beard burns on my changing face in the light of day. Sometimes when you step out of bed, the blood returns to your head and the world looks as if it has changed without you.

"I sent some of your paintings off for a scholarship. I'll pay for the rest of the tuition."

Raúl stands up and starts taking off his shirt and then his pants. I watch hypnotized by the cruelty that only belongs to the young and beautiful.

"No, no, none of that."

Raúl sits down dejected. "So are you divorced now?"

This makes me howl, "No, Mia is too Catholic for that!"

He joins with his own laughter. "I miss painting on the beach. Everything felt so sinful."

"It will again . . . in art school."

Raúl asks, "What are you watching?"

"Shit."

"When did you know? About yourself?"

I'm not sure what he is asking. About being an artist? Being gay? Being unafraid of nudes safe within frames? Of belonging to a species that rarely lives beyond a century?

"I'm the mystery that the rest of the world has long figured out."

Raúl nods and settles back, "Put the television on a little louder."

"You'll have plenty of fools at art school that'll want to talk about philosophy and other vital matters to the soul."

He leans forward and places a kiss on my lips. "You are not old, Arturo."

"And you are very young. It's not fair."

"Sssh," Raúl responds, "I think the hunk is going to swim naked in the sea."

"It's television. They won't show much."

"Ah," interrupts the painter that will someday be admired and honored in ways that I will never be. "Crumbs are a feast for the starving."

"Some man better kick that romanticism out of your heart."

We watch the magical blue screen, two painters in a town that may survive as footnotes to Raúl's talents. He says, "May I paint you someday, Arturo?"

"Yes, of course, Raúl, but first I need a few new secrets so that you may find me a challenge."

I excuse myself and walk up the stairs, sit at the top of them. I see the blue light flicker like a cold fire that is incapable of burning down the house that has accidentally become a home. Nothing has prepared me for this profound happiness.

Rat Poison: The Book of Marcus Mar

1. Now that he has mailed off his suicide note to friends and enemies, he can relax.

2. It is so strange to look at his apartment in such disorder and to feel as if he might burst into laughter.

3. Yes, *burst* is the word, for surely flower buds burst into a landscape, for Spring is a violence.

4. The space heater glows like a Cyclops in heat.

5. He watches the red for awhile, and tries to notice how long it takes before he gets bored.

6. There is so much that he doesn't know about himself, about his body.

7. He sits in each chair in his apartment and becomes overwhelmed by their differences under his thin ass that he goes to his bed to be comforted by the familiar.

8. His blankets smell of him.

9. Is that what he really smells like?

10. He doesn't want to read a book and he is tired of always reading the palms of his trembling hands.

11. Thank God that he isn't in love at the moment for then Time might regain its importance in what little life is dripping through his veins; Time might have a hostage with a first name.

12. One of his few regrets is that he has never really understood even one thief's heart, that most thieves are actually very practical dreamers.

13. He fantasizes that someone is breaking into his place and that he tells the burglar that he is the last human he will ever see.

14. God, he is going to miss his eyes.

15. He counts his toes ten times until the numbers come to have a meaning.

16. His toes look like family pets that are unknowingly being lovingly raised for distant holiday meals.

17. Is everything a tragedy?

18. The Greeks had their satyr plays.

19. He could drink rum while singing along to the *West Side Story* soundtrack as some kind of ironic gesture, but with his death so close the absence of an audience gains importance.

20. He admires the beauty of his night table's curving legs, Cleopatra as a quadruplet.

21. The last thing he wants to do is to think about his Life, but Life is cruel enough to be visible at the most inconvenient times.

22. He farts because he has taken too many deep breaths.

23. Amazing how the seams of one's underwear are so undervalued.

24. He stares into an apple that he bit into just yesterday, and now looks like a wound surrounded by red skin.

25. He is done with eating.

26. He wishes he had been crazy enough to rename himself—rebaptize himself with one of those million bottles of champagne that had been bought in his honor—so that he might recklessly exit this world as John-the-Beloved, Jr., or something as equally spectacular.

27. Which of his friends or enemies would be the first to open up his suicide note?

28. Who are his friends and enemies?

29. Has he truly been anyone's friend?

30. He stares at a canceled postage stamp and it looks like a poem written nervously by some mad eunuch.

31. He opens the window, the only window in his bedroom.

32. It is above his head, and as far as it has been reported, it still remains in that apartment.

33. The air is like a hat, only more pure, and less susceptible to being shaped by any passing head.

34. He smells mud from blocks away.

35. He wonders how long it will take before rain seeps into his bones.

36. *Not yet*, he tells himself, *but soon enough*.

37. His Cubs cap looks ridiculous against his blue jeans nailed into the bedroom wall.

38. While he is not to leave a son or daughter behind, the semblance of a scarecrow hanging on a nail, instead of a Christ, makes him laugh aloud.

39. He wonders if the excitement he is feeling is a symptom of the rat poison and so he counts his heartbeats as if they are roses paid for by someone else, a long-awaited stranger.

40. Consistency is rather Gothic in our quantum science society, although once our deaths cancel out our privileges as a living citizen, why then consistency is reduced into a retrospective show, a photo album, a story or two, a drunk tale, a happening long happened.

41. He grabs a nearby envelope, licks it until spit covers his face like some Renaissance beard.

42. He seals air inside that envelope, letter to himself in the grave.

43. He smells it.

44. He crushes it into a white flower and throws it out through the opened window so that it might have the chance to root outside of his consciousness.

45. How has he become so literary?

46. He tries to imagine that Christ is smothering him against His holy chest.

47. Gasping, he lays still, only to learn that lightbulbs sing to themselves all the time, all that time.

48. Why is he without a mother or father?

49. He sings along with the lightbulb.

50. He feels such tremendous joy knowing that he won't live to pay the electric bill.

51. He thinks he should be dead by now, but he has never been very fortunate.

52. *Not yet*, he says aloud.

53. Does the Russian *nyet* mean *not yet*?

54. He tries pissing but to see his sex is to bring back memories not quite distant enough to be pleasant or overwhelmingly positive.

55. What is self-control about?

56. He looks closely at the scar on his inside right thigh.

57. Either it has grown smaller or else he has grown beyond his old pains.

58. He starts to wonder just then what his jacket might do without him, his body, his stink.

59. Stink is a garden without a gardener.

60. He drinks rum and can't stop himself from playing the *West Side Story* soundtrack until it becomes too painful to think about thinking and not thinking.

61. He never has returned the library book, *In the Palaces of Memory*.

62. He has to forget his life.

63. The rat poison has graciously offered him no other choice.

64. Choices he had made were always underpinned by someone else's ideas of *normality*.

65. Trying to find someone to blame by name makes him sleepy.

66. Certainly his sleeping has something to do with forgetting that he himself will never comprehend the universe even as it simultaneously comprehends him.

67. He concentrates on his neck's strange pleasure from pressing against the zebra-striped pillows.

68. A neighbor's phone rings and rings.

69. He listens to it as if some angel is writing him a love letter of sound.

70. He wonders if his body is really transforming food into shit even as he is dying.

71. He feels the urge to order pizza from every pizzeria in the phone book and laughs at the image of seeing millions of pizza men and women trying to knock down his door while wearing an aromatic

halo of *the works*: garlic, mushrooms, tomatoes, green peppers, extra cheese, pineapple and spinach.

72. Maybe he should have shaved himself with a straight razor.

73. Maybe he has; he feels his chin in order to confirm the past.

74. He waits for the rat poison to ride up his brain stem as if a flower bud pushing into a rainy morning and by waiting he learns that his body is exceptionally good at keeping secrets from him.

75. He is still more alive than dead.

76. Is he still himself?

77. He hopes the little fuckers who found him pretentious while living will be up to their noses in the shit he is leaving behind.

78. Sincerity gives the impression that one must have manners that require one to be in a tuxedo.

79. *Ok. Ok. Ok. Ok. Ok. Ok. Ok. Ok. Ok. OK?*

80. He wonders why elbows are so ugly and unlovable.

81. A mosquito died in a cup of coffee he has not finished because he doesn't want to take the edge off his rum.

82. He does nothing for many seconds.

83. He doesn't feel good.

84. Is that a sign that Death will possess him soon enough?

85. He reaches for more rum—damn you, coffee—even though he doesn't want to romanticize these last moments.

86. He touches his sex but it has died long before the rest of him has.

87. A picture of a naked man on the East wall embarrasses him with its effusive engineering wonders.

88. The naked man's head is turned toward something out of the frame, out of the room, out of the city, out of the world, out of history.

89. The nude's left arm looks like a pincher far from the sea, tragic evolutionist.

90. The photo doesn't smell of anything, but he does.

91. He wishes he had a comrade that would at least shut his eyes after his death.

92. He can't stop coughing.

93. He cups his balls because the ache in them is an old puberty.

94. He bends over.

95. He wears the body of his birth to the burning grave in his head.

96. He had imagined that this whole business would have been quicker and much more silent.

97. He lays on the floor, spreads his arms and legs and seeks mercy like that given to furniture by ghosts.

98. The cold floor soaks into his bones.

99. He looks up into heaven's crotch.

100. He has never taken a good look at his ceiling before and he loves this world that doesn't love him.

101. It is an uncarved tombstone, an eternity of whiteness.

Lois and Her Supermen

I gave One-Juan his name.

His real name is Juan.

We met at a party where the Hostess, a drag queen decked out like Queen Victoria in a leather mini, proclaimed that I had just returned from Puerto Rico and lived to tell it since there were so few 5-Star hotels in that forsaken place.

"Ah," I said, "but there were more than five stars in the sky."

I actually got applause for that response, because that was a time when AIDS and death were thought to be a paranoid's wet dream.

Juan was not as handsome in those days and so safe from diseases, or at least, this was the theory he eventually shared with me.

He was skinny, in a torn T-shirt; his retro-Brando biker look is never truly out of fashion.

Juan said he was Puerto Rican.

It turned out that was the way he always introduced himself, as if expecting for someone to say someday, "You look like one."

I said, "Oh, another one. Tony Orlando is one. Rita Moreno is one. You're One-Juan."

He had made me nervous and I liked that enough to pretend not to care.

"I like that. Call me One-Juan."

He leaned over and I could smell him, like a garden that's between blossoming and falling apart. "And you?"

"I'm Lois."

"Oh," he smiled that now famous One-Juan smile, "What an old-fashioned name. How delightful! What a magical childhood you must have had."

I wanted to make love to him there, in front of everyone.

"No, actually," I answered, "I was named after Superman's

girlfriend, Lois. Not Lana. Lana is Superman's girl of the past. I'm the future, honey, always."

"Magic is magic," One-Juan replied, bowing.

He disappeared into the crowd.

But I found him because one of us is the magnet and one of us is the lead; we tend to take turns at power.

So many friends blame my relationships with men on my relationship with my father.

If it was only that simple.

Sometimes I think the United States has over-analyzed itself.

I was watching the news yesterday when a cop was being interviewed about a man who had pickled the hearts of six women.

"He came from a dysfunctional family," the calm man of order said into the microphone, into the camera, into my living room, into my head.

"Show me your damn psychology degree." I screamed, throwing the *People* magazine at him, but of course he wasn't there.

One-Juan was there at that party, present in our ever intimate conversation.

He has this uncanny talent for listening.

One-Juan casually told me he was a bisexual.

I laughed, thinking of a limerick I knew about a bicycle built for two that was ridden into the bushes by one.

One-Juan.

He had never been to Puerto Rico and really couldn't speak Spanish—but he understood it from growing up with transvestites like me. "Lois, you make me speak in tongues."

I felt sorry for him. "You're like a mute, in some ways."

He nodded.

I remember wondering if One-Juan wore underwear or not.

He didn't let me find out right away.

"You act," I said, "like you're a prince when you're nobody at all."

We fought from the very first.

He laughed back at me, finally giving him the opportunity. "Shows how much you know. America has no prince."

One-Juan stuffed his hands into his dream jeans.

"Hah!" I smiled. "What about John-John Kennedy! Huh, One-Juan? Talk about Prince Charming!"

I was trying to hurt him in the ego, a place as vulnerable as any man's crotch.

"You win."

I hadn't been trying to defeat One-Juan.

I turned to him and said, "Juan, you're the One-Juan of Puerto Rico."

I leaned against him. "I'm a crazy, Miss Clairol, red-headed woman. Better than the real thing. And if you think of yourself as coming from the first family of Puerto Rico, you can be that. You might even marry into it."

"Not unless the Governor has an ungovernable son," the man smiled, "I'm bisexual but I sleep with men."

"The whole island," I hissed, "is ungovernable. That's why you and I are going there together!"

From that day on, he introduced himself as One-Juan and no one said too much about it.

Even his old friends started to call him that.

One time, One-Juan did get angry when a man said, "Yeah, sure, and I'm Bam-Bam."

And One-Juan did bam him, in the alley.

One-Juan had taken care of himself since he was seventeen years-old and claimed that he hasn't trusted anyone until me.

We moved in together as friends and only once did I leave him alone for more than one night.

He was always fascinated by my transformation from Louie, the florist, into Lois, the heartbreaker.

One-Juan actually looked sad the day I had to leave town because my father was dying in Miami.

"One-Juan, don't screw in my bed. It's RSVP, only, babe. Got that?"

He was walking around in his underwear, trying to look like some deserted child.

"And don't show me yourself unless it means you're giving me a going-away present I'll never forget!"

Embarrassed at being so obvious, One-Juan put on some clothes.

He walked me to my car and kissed me.

I felt like a bride, who was going to her sick father for permission to be happy. "One-Juan, I'm a little scared."

He leaned into the car, stroked my cheek. "Honey, most of us would be giant scared. You are the bravest woman I know."

I leaned forward, accidentally hitting the car horn. "I'm the only woman you know."

He smiled at me. "Remember that song. There is no beast without the beauty?"

"You screw-up," I laughed, crying. "It's the other way around."

He moved his eyebrows up and down and I didn't say goodbye, fare thee well, hasta la vista, ciao.

Nothing.

■ ■ ■

I drove and drove.

Right before Miami the headlights of my car caught palm trees bobbing in the wind.

A damn thunderstorm.

I pulled over to the side, listened to Oral Roberts so I could have someone to argue with, and wondered if Father was dying this time.

He had tried so many times before.

Father answered the door when I got to my brother's house.

"Hi, it's Lewie. I'm here."

He looked up at me, puzzled.

I noticed that his silver hair shine had been dulled by some hair gel.

He cleared his throat and said calmly, "The wind is speaking to me. And put your make-up back on. I prefer you as Lois. A dying man needs beauty."

With this proclamation, he turned away, went inside.

I followed.

That was the visit where I learned to write pornography.

It began when Father decided that he wanted me to write out his epitaph because my brother Ernesto was a bore (and he remains one to this day).

"You're the artist," Father insisted.

"Dad, I just airbrush album covers. That's it."

"Lois, listen to me," he said. "Ernesto only knows how to go to work, sign his name on his paycheck, give it to wife, and then go back to work. If I left it to Ernesto, the newspaper would publish my epitaph as one huge signature, two columns wide."

I knew I had lost the argument.

Still, I tried. "You're exaggerating."

He sat on his bed. "Am I? Ernesto's children have to read the *TV Guide* to him! Ha!"

I didn't get along with Ernesto, but then only his wife Vivian did.

How long would that last?

Father and I agreed that I would take notes the next morning and prepare his epitaph.

"Even if it's not published, it can be read at the services."

I went to sleep, after giving up on finding any alcohol in the house.

Years later, I found out Vivian kept bottles of stuff up in the attic.

Perhaps the madwoman in the attic is only a drunk.

I hope so.

The next morning, Father couldn't remember the exact date of his birth and I knew it was a hint of the trouble to come.

"Put down June 1st," he said. "I had my first sexual experience on a June 1st. That I remember!"

"Which century?" I asked wryly.

Then Father went on and on.

The epitaph became a biography of sorts and I found myself writing into the afternoon and promising to resume the next day.

I protested after each additional page; after page 23 I knew I didn't know much about this man. "They'll only give you four sentences and only if the newspaper hasn't sold enough advertisement space."

Father just sat there, wrapped in an Indian blanket Vivian had bought during her hippie stage.

"Now Lois, I'm ready to talk about what I call my Red Light district phase. Don't be shocked, but your father was a man!"

I stared at him dumbly.

"A man, Lois."

"Yeah, and?" I yawned.

"Don't yawn, Lois. There are people in this world who I hope you never meet that mistake an open mouth for an invitation. Now, make sure you write down every word. I'm going to read these notes to make sure you're not a liar like Ernesto."

I protested. "Ernesto isn't a liar."

"No, he isn't that smart. But he is lied to, and often. Then he shares what he thinks is truth and becomes an accidental liar. Pitiful."

So our collaboration began.

I wrote about the woman who kept a parrot on her brass bed because she felt in a past life she had killed a crying baby.

I read back to him the story of the woman who tattooed her breasts so to resemble two huge eyes which she came to call the Prophets of God.

I faithfully recorded the tale about his best friend's wife who slept with him out of revenge because her husband had lost his right hand glove she had bought for him for no special occasion.

"It was made out of sheepskin," Father emphasized.

I grew bored by Father's list of sexual conquests.

Mother had died when I was ten so I had long ago assumed Father had had sex with strangers, but his stories were incredible.

I began to add details.

I changed names.

I invented positions.

I insisted that I read the notes at the end of our sessions just to see if Father might notice my changes.

He was never shocked.

I wanted to shock him.

I had Father shave off the pubic hair of a Maternity Ward nurse.

I had him tie up my first grade teacher to our picket fence and thrash her with silk stockings until Miss Jenkins begged him to use her any which way.

Father fell asleep on that one.

Perhaps if I had tied him to the fence instead.

I wrote feverishly.

For every sentence Father gave me, I added four, then five, until I finally wasn't writing down one word he was saying to me.

Days before he died, I shocked him.

I had written a story about him being alone at home.

Greta Garbo was on the TV.

He leaned forward and kissed her, trying to jump inside her eyes.

Father wept.

His shoulders shook.

His face grew puffed as a frog's throat.

"That never happened. That would be like raping the mother of God."

That night, Father came into my room and said, "I wish I was dying in a desert."

I put on my robe, opened the window.

It was a clear night.

I remember that it was a clear night, like in that Christmas song "It Came Upon a Midnight Clear."

I always thought that song would be great on a soundtrack for a Dracula movie.

"Lois, it's so sad to die without music."

I didn't know what to say.

"When you're in love," he said, "you hear music. I do. I did."

I pulled him to me and rocked him as if he was a little boy. "Daddy, why do you want to be in a desert?"

He looked at me, as if I was an idiot. "Because I never did go to Egypt. I promised myself I would. But I didn't."

What could I say?

I rocked him and sang to him my latest favorite song:

I was there with my eyes
wide open
hoping you'd recognize me
by the tears
in my eyes
and don't say
don't say
don't say you don't remember
I gave you
my telephone number

Father smiled at me and said, "Ernesto would have sang me 'My Bonnie lies over the Ocean' or some other shit."

I had to ask. "Does he hold you? Treat you good?"

Father settled in my arms, mumbling, "Ernesto is the child I made with your Mother because we were so in love. He has to treat me good."

I bit my lip. "And me, Father?"

"You, Lois, I made you, we made you, we tried for you. It took months. Yeah, making love can be damn hard work."

I wished I believed in ghosts because I actually looked around the room in case my mother was standing in that room that very minute.

She wasn't, of course.

"You were our present to the world. Ernesto was an act of selfishness. We wanted you to make a difference. Like Superman's girlfriend, I said to your mother and she laughed at me."

I had heard this story before and wanted to hear it again.

"What difference is that, Papi?"

He reached his hand out in the air and pretended to catch the moonlight coming in the window.

"Why, Louis, after Lois Lane. Lois Lane was the first career girl I knew!"

We laughed together.

I asked him if he had any regrets and he just said he wished he had lived a less sober life.

I told him about One-Juan but he didn't want to know.

"Look at me. I already have too much to carry into my grave."

And then he died soon after that heart-to-heart.

Death is more complex for the living.

For Vivian, for example.

She was the one who still talks about Father's face turned away from the window.

"As if he had seen enough."

I've wanted to respond to that for years, that Vivian was obviously ignorant of the law of gravity, that the earth's spin simply pulled Father's head one way instead of another.

I've kept silent because who am I to rewrite Vivian's story?

Ernesto turned out to be wonderful during the entire burial.

He took care of everything and even Vivian looked at her husband in a new way.

Father went with the wind like some drifting seed hoping to blossom in a kinder and gentler world without politicians, without religious leaders—in other words, a land of lovers, paradise unclaimed.

■ ■ ■

I hurried back home only to find One-Juan in my bed with the TV on.

He was watching *Bewitched* reruns.

"Dr. Bombay is trying to cure Samantha of witchitis or something."

I asked him why he was in my bed, naked.

"I could smell you in your sheets."

I collapsed.

He took me in his arms, brought me to the bed and held me, held me, held me so I wouldn't fall off the edge of the world suddenly gone flat, the flat earth, flattened Earth.

I kissed him and he kissed me back.

"Are you trying to make love to me?" I whispered.

"I'm not trying. I am making love to me."

He licked my neck.

Put his hand up my skirt.

I had been waiting for so long for that.

My hand rubbed against the front of him.

He pressed back.

I held him.

He didn't push me away.

I stopped him as he started to pull my panties down.

"Am I not doing it right?"

"One-Juan, listen. Once an illusion is ruined, it's ruined forever."

I pulled his head up so that it could be next to mine.

I could feel his eyelashes against my cheekbones.

"I want to wait."

"Hey, Lois, lightning has struck, ok?"

He pressed his shaking hands against my crotch and no amount of thinking could stop my erection from poking out of my panties.

"I wish two men could make a child because it would be born out of our fierceness."

Athena, our daughter.

My father's dead forever.

One-Juan smiled at me.

"We're not making a child today. We're making you."

I stretched out. "Let's just watch the Stevenses and see if a woman who is a witch can love a man that's a mortal."

One-Juan wrapped the sheets around me tenderly.

He stood up and he was beautiful. "Are you sure?"

He posed as if for some porno photographer.

"I'm sure. You're my friend. I'm not in love with you anymore. I just love you."

"Just like that?"

I nodded and he looked bewildered for a moment, then laughed.

"I'm glad you told me because I'm freezing without my clothes. I just wanted to make sure you weren't hurting. I only know how to make people feel good."

I sent him off to put on the Indiana Jones and the Temple of Doom pajamas I bought him for Valentines' Day.

One-Juan, though clumsy, cared about me.

Would he come to my death-bed and make me laugh?

Or will tragedy be the only meal I can ask for by name?

I hope not.

I hope I can hope.

I don't know.

One-Juan whistles "The Yellow Rose of Texas" in the kitchen.

He must have eaten at Taco Bell everyday while I was gone.

The song was a good choice.

The sun is sinking into its golden nest in the west.

I'm more bewildered than bewitched right now.

I'm a cave bursting with jewels that even Ali Baba hasn't discovered yet.

Someone's in the Kitchen with José

Friends at the interrupted party stared at me more out of curiosity than concern. Not everyone is privileged to witness a man's reaction on hearing of his mother's death. I had been expecting her death for such a long time that I was emptied of any public and important gestures. How tempting it was to make a grand toast to my mother. I could have lit any number of candles I always keep around the house in case of a fierce thunderstorm and loss of power. Instead, I mumbled something and fled to the kitchen.

Slowly the party recovered from its blow.

Indeed it seemed as if the party fed off the blood of my dead mother; the sounds that came from the various rooms were excessive and almost bordering abandonment. It was strange to be hiding from my own party. Friends came to the kitchen for ice, food, for the chance to stare at me as if I was a car accident and they were rubbernecking. Why had I selected the kitchen, of all the rooms in my house, as my refuge?

Mother had never been a very good cook and so I wasn't being nostalgic for a place filled with the smells of onions cooking in garlic oil or Spanish rice with peas. I poured myself a gin and tonic and relaxed at the small breakfast table that I had bought at a flea market on the edge of town. It was red, like an apple, Satan's back, an overturned toy firetruck.

■ ■ ■

Father told Mother that he had fucked Julia, Mother's greatest enemy on Sun Street. With one sweep of his left arm, he knocked the salt and pepper shakers off the table. He lacked the finesse of Jack Nicholson in *The Postman Always Rings Twice* and perhaps this may explain why Mother just stared at me as if he was merely a misbehaving child. I watched them closely as if a televised baseball game—the slow pace itself central to the game.

"How could you do that to me?" Mother eventually said, "Now I can't hate her. I have no choice but to feel sorry for her. The way I feel sorry for myself."

Father, accustomed to Mother's monologues, had taken advantage of the dramatic pause and statement to go to the refrigerator for a beer.

As he recrossed the kitchen to return to his post by the sink, Father tripped over my feet.

I instinctively held onto him as we both fell to the floor.

"I just was trying to open the beer for you," I said in my little voice.

Father sat on the floor, sweeping me into his arms.

I was suddenly his shield from Mother.

"Go on, son, open the beer can."

Father had taught me that the sound of a beer can being opened was the echo of an invisible bullet being shot out into space, a magic bullet that could shoot down stars.

"We help God kill the old stars so he can make new shiny ones."

I shot at yet another star even as Mother hit me on the head. "Get out of here. Your father and I have to talk."

I didn't want to leave my Father's warm embrace but he gently pushed me toward the doorway.

I ran up to my room and closed the door.

This didn't stop the noise of the terrible storm that thundered and roared in our kitchen from entering my room and my ears.

Later on it was my chore to sweep up the broken dishes and drinking glasses.

Once again a hurricane had hit our house.

Is naming one after ourselves a challenge to God?

I tried doing a good job, fearful that in the middle of some night I or someone in the family would split open a foot from an overlooked broken piece of glass.

I didn't want anything to be my fault, not if I could help it.

■ ■ ■

Joe looked out of his kitchen window at the birdfeeder he had cleverly set up, tied around the streetlight that lit up his apartment patio and parking lot.

His stillness disturbed me. "It's midnight. There are no birds outside."

"Maybe I'll catch an angel at the birdfeeder."

"Come on, Joe. What's wrong?"

"Wrong?"

"Well, what's right?"

"Right?"

He shrugged, "Angels got to eat and keep their strength. It's tiring work battling the evils of this world."

"Joe?"

So many terrible scenarios crossed my mind, most of them centered around AIDS.

Had Joe finally slept with the wrong male lover?

Was I going to lose my best friend so unexpectedly?

I mentally accused myself of being selfish: Joe's tragedy was not mine.

I am not the center of the universe.

This has always been a difficult lesson to learn.

"I know. I know. But this isn't easy."

I looked around as if looking for ghosts. "Hey, it's me. Painting this ceiling wasn't easy. Talking to me is, should be. You know that."

"Do you mean it?"

"Joe?"

He took a deep breath and said slowly, "I'm gay."

I shrugged, "And?"

"You're not shocked?"

"I was a little bit about a year ago when I first suspected you were."

"It was obvious?"

"No. Yes. I don't know. Why are you telling me now?"

Joe didn't answer me; instead he poured us a new cup of coffee.

Early Spring had proven to be raw.

I have always loved the word "raw."

Once in the grocery store I felt as if I had hit the jackpot when I discovered bags and bags of raw sugar.

I felt like a pirate with a chest of gold.

"Wait, there's more," Joe said in a strange voice that returned me to that time and place in a hurry.

I was a little impatient, ready to go out on our usual rounds about town on a Saturday night.

I looked at him directly. "It's OK Joe. We've been friends because . . . . we're friends."

"I'm in love with you."

I dropped the coffee cup and it shattered on the tiled floor.

Joe shrank back and then suddenly ran out of the kitchen.

Once again I found myself kneeling and picking up pieces of an unexpected storm.

Why had I reacted the way I did?

Had I been sending Joe the wrong messages?

Was I somehow culpable in his misreading our friendship?

Was I secretly in love with him too?

Was I afraid of being a homosexual?

Was I still afraid of my father?

Joe returned with a broom and a dustpan in his shaking hands.

He bowed his head and said, "Forget I ever told you that. I'm drunk."

"We were drinking coffee."

"I'm high."

"You don't do drugs."

"I'm stupid."

"Your IQ is bigger than mine."

"Hey, you're not goddam Darwin you know."

"I don't love you like that, Joe. But I love you. Just not like that? OK, buddy?"

Joe pretended to be angry. "And why the hell not? Is it my coffee? Is my coffee that bad?"

I relaxed as Joe acted normal once again.

The word "normal" had to be tossed out of my vocabulary as soon as possible.

We stepped out into the night and we talked about everything but each other.

I got drunk and Joe, as usual, was the designated driver.

I trusted him with my life.

If I could ever love a man, it would be Joe, José, my working class hero, banana revolutionary, desperado without a credit card, Joe the Ho Ho Ho Man, matador of my heart, Joe.

He used to be José when we were children.

He had never once failed to return me back to my house, back to the ghosts from my childhood who waited for me like jealous pets.

■ ■ ■

Abraham Lincoln's house in Springfield, Illinois was smaller than I imagined that such a tall Republican president would have required.

Of course the railings to keep tourists from actually entering the rooms, the plastic carpeting in the hallways and the crowds themselves didn't contribute much to the sense of architectural space.

It was only on the second floor, in the Irish maid's plain bedroom, that I felt a chill pass through me.

It was like my mother's room, also next to the staircase that led directly to the kitchen.

We were led there next and I stared at the black woodburning stove but it lent neither questions or visions.

How strange that moment was when I realized that viewpoints of history depend on who gets to be the servant and who gets to be the master.

■ ■ ■

Mother was obsessed with the kitchen curtains and would secretly buy new ones at K-Mart every two to three weeks.

She would sing as she took off the old curtains and folded them into perfect squares which were then hidden away in baskets and boxes in the basements.

My favorite song that she sang was *Moon River* for when Mother sang it, she would seem young, as if anticipating something that hadn't entered her life yet; she had a nice voice.

After a year's worth of curtains, Mother would drop them off at the Salvation Army or Goodwill, proudly announcing to the workers on the docks, "They're like new."

Of course Father knew about the curtains but he said nothing about them.

He had been raised to think that a woman happy with her kitchen was bound to be one happy wife.

He kept hoping that Mother's happiness would kick in soon, that she would accompany him to the bars once again, that he could stay at home in peace.

He waited for signs of happiness at each dinner but Mother's cooking never improved.

Once Father caught me cooking.

I was sixteen and trying to expand my role as peacemaker at home.

I was convinced that I had solved Mother's cooking problems: she was always too much in a hurry and never allowed the food to simmer in their own juices.

She never even cut onions so they were in small circles, like wedding rings; Mother would chop the onions into four huge pieces and just throw them into that night's dinner.

All her meals were like stews for giants.

"What are you doing?" Father asked in a slow, low voice.

"Helping out."

"Where is she? More goddam curtains?"

"Probably," I nodded.

Father tugged at me. "Come with me. For one moment. Go on and put the pan on low flame."

"I'll turn it off."

"Whatever."

There was something strange in father's voice, something I had never heard before.

It didn't make me so much afraid but curious.

I followed him to the backyard.

He put his arm around me and whispered, "Son, you gotta get the hell out of this house. And soon, OK?"

This intimacy frightened me.

I pulled away but Father refused to let me go.

"I'm not good enough to be your Father, am I?"

"No, it's just that. . ."

Without warning he raised his left fist and brought it hard against my nose.

Father let me go and I staggered backwards.

Father hit me with his right fist again but this time I managed to turn my head away from him.

I thought about running inside but the screendoor was closed and I knew I would lose precious moments grabbing for the doorknob.

"Hit me you son-of-a-bitch. Hit me."

I so wanted to but I was afraid of this man who suddenly wasn't my father.

I swung and missed him.

I swung again.

He dropped both of his arms and pressed his face forward. "Come on, a free shot."

I took it and hit Father in the face as hard as I could.

He staggered backwards and fell to the grass.

I jumped at him, crying and bleeding.

I wanted to hit him again, to bury his face in the grass.

Instead I helped him up, embracing him.

If I don't let him get enough room to swing his arms. . . .

Father held me and then pushed me away.

"One day you'll thank me for this."

I walked slowly into the house, grabbed a kitchen towel and filled it up with ice.

My face burned.

Father came in and took a look at his handiwork.

His nose was bleeding and he threw his head back.

We stayed in our corners for several minutes when Mother suddenly came in.

She quickly hid two K-Mart bags in a drawer and then screamed when she took a good look at me.

"My God, what happened here?"

I said, "Nothing."

"That's right woman. This is what nothing looks like."

"It's ugly too," I added.

Suddenly Father and I were laughing as if I had said the funniest thing in the world.

He walked over and put his arm around me.

I fell against him.

I loved this man as much as I hated him.

Mother sensed that something strange and perhaps important had occurred.

She took advantage by telling us to wash up and to get dressed for dinner.

"I was making dinner," I protested.

Mother wasn't about to give up a trip to *Ponderosa* without a fight. "This kitchen smells like a locker room. It's unhealthy to eat here until it's all been aired out. Go on, the two of you open the windows here and then go and shower."

We admired her ingenuity and looked at each other, smiling as if we were sharing a secret.

Perhaps we did, only I didn't understand it.

"Come on son," Father said in an amused voice, "Let your mother put up her fucking curtains in peace."

■ ■ ■

Mother had been dead for about six months when Father wanted me to go out for a drink with him.

I kept waiting for some surprise announcement, some crisis, some confidence.

It turned out that Father wanted a drinking companion that night and that was all.

I was disappointed but accepted the situation as normal.

"It's nice to have a son that doesn't get too moral," he said slowly.

I wasn't used to praise from him.

What was I being praised for?

■ ■ ■

Alberto loved the sound of his voice in bars for he had long accepted the fact that he was not a talented poet or even a mediocre computer salesman.

He replaced talent and ambition with loudness.

Alberto had always been merely a companion who always spent lots of money on drinks and music.

I sought him out whenever I felt emptied out by my job as a data entry clerk and needed a distraction from my own thoughts, boredom.

Like Mother, Alberto loved his monologues.

Perhaps I surrounded myself with talkers because they relieved me from most of the responsibilities of shepherding Silence.

"I bet you don't know where most women fantasize making love?" Alberto asked.

After guessing a church, a barn, a limousine, Alberto screamed throughout the bar, "They love fucking on their own kitchen floors!"

"I don't believe it."

"Think about it. What better place to get revenge on both your mother and your father. It's a Freudian thing. Me, I don't like the kitchen floor. I look around and see dust bunnies multiplying underneath the stove, the refrigerator. Sometimes table legs are wrapped up with cobwebs like some transparent fur coat. Shit, I'll do it on the kitchen floor if I have to. But I like a bed. I've done it outside and every single goddamn time I wake up with mosquito bites. And I mean all over the place. I like a bed but if it's the kitchen floor or nothing then I'm the mop of their desires, the broom of their need. I don't buy that Freud shit but it gives us a name for wanting to do it until we stop hurting. I think it's ancient, hombre. Older than everything. Need is and if you got to be ass down on a floor that smells of other people's feet, why then that's proof that it controls us, and not we it. Whatever it is that makes women push up against you."

"Alberto, you're crazy."

"And you're sane? No, thanks."

I ordered us a new round.

Alberto pretended to look for his wallet but I threw some money on the table.

"It's for us."

"It's not like I'm not giving you something in return. The kitchen floor. Man, someday you and your joystick will thank me for this."

The bartender walked over, gave us our Rolling Rock and Budweiser and then asked Alberto to lower his voice, "There are ladies present and they want to claw out your eyes. That's not covered by my insurance, comprende?"

Alberto went on and on until I stopped seeing him for I noticed a woman at a table all by herself, a blonde who probably was born a brunette.

I ended up laughing with her, laughter that seemed to be coming straight from the heart of my groin.

■ ■ ■

Father went to Mother's wake with his girlfriend, Estrella.

She stayed in the car during the service, the car running so the air conditioner could keep her beauty crisp and untouched by the summer or by death.

The drunk relatives were spurred by this unexpected soap opera and began yelling curses at Father but he ignored them; I followed him into a side room.

It was the kitchen where the caterers were preparing a somber meal for themselves; death doesn't stop others from being hungry or from feeding themselves.

He took me in his arms and we wept together.

My father was always the soft one, the romantic one.

My mother was now the dead one.

Father pretended to throw me a punch and said, "I'm going to leave. This is your family. Not mine. Are you going to be OK?"

I nodded, looking around at the three workers eating their lunch.

I wanted to give God the finger, the way he so often did to me.

We walked to the car but the storm had broken there while Father and I had made our peace.

My Grandmother Lucy was hitting the car's passenger's window with her useless fists, "Puta, puta."

Uncle Carlos was screaming at Estrella and at Grandmother Lucy.

Cousin Carmen stood in front of our car and waving her arms, "Don't you respect the dead? Wait until you are one, querida!"

Others were laughing.

Others were crying.

Father ran towards the car, screaming.

I watched him sit in the car, embrace Estrella.

He honked and honked the horn, started the car, and drove backwards out of the cul-de-sac.

The bastard, he left me behind.

Papi left me behind.

Everyone returned to the funeral wearing adrenaline's best pink.

Mother had been forgotten, and we looked at her body as if it already had overstayed its invitation.

I didn't cry that night.

I didn't do anything except sit in the backyard and listen to the stars sing to each other of tragedies greater than my own.

■ ■ ■

The women I seem to date are very independent; I did not want my mother back in my life under any circumstances.

Linda and I became friends after she became pregnant with another man's baby just two weeks after we broke up.

Rita gave me an appointment notebook so we could coordinate our dates.

Sleepovers were easier than actual evenings spent in a restaurant or club.

Judy was beautiful and it became frustrating to see a parade of men trying to pick her up during our dates.

She was gracious, gentle but how to forgive that one time I saw her slip her phone number into a handsome man's hands?

Gillian, a twin, warned me from the start that she had been divorced twice and so she doubted we could ever become a couple.

We lived together for 40 days; I call that my Noah's Ark love.

Alice married Alberto and I did look at their kitchen floor when I came to my first nervous visit.

Alberto laughed at me, "You lost a good thing here, buddy."

Was I destined to be alone?

■ ■ ■

Mother said gingerbread men were really men and that everyone in our family was a cannibal.

Stunned, I watched her face closely to see if she was telling the truth or not.

"Don't tell the boy that," my Father growled. "Let him stay a kid a little longer."

"Who the hell do you think you are? Charlton Heston?"

The tone of her voice sent chills down my spine; a new hurricane without a name was being born even as we had so innocently been enjoying Sunday morning.

"I didn't mean anything by it," Father howled in return.

They were experienced at their roles as water and wind.

It was too late; Mother couldn't hear him.

She started to scream, tearing off her blouse.

My Father grabbed her but she refused him and tangled herself up in the kitchen curtains, new ones.

I knew my cue.

I went upstairs to my room.

I listened to see if the hurricane had followed me upstairs.

An hour or so later, I went downstairs and found my parents sitting on the couch, kissing.

I retreated but refused to be a prisoner in my bedroom any longer.

I snuck out of the house through the kitchen door.

The world was waiting for me.

I never ate a gingerbread man since that Sunday.

■ ■ ■

Holly loved asking stupid questions in bed. "What's your favorite food? I mean, if the Nazis had asked you what you wanted for your last meal, what would it be?"

I was naked, sweaty and exhausted by my long life. "If I was a French Resistance guy that got caught, I'd ask for French fries."

"Seriously."

"Tuna casserole."

"That's stupid."

"Yeah, thanks."

"It's stupid. It's not romantic. You're not romantic. Joe is. I wish you were Joe."

I turned off the light by my side of the bed. "He's fucking gay."

"I know."

"And?"

"He doesn't want my apples. I know that much, silly."

I gave her my best I'm-disgusted-with-you-cockroach look, "That's because he wants my apples."

Holly jumped out of bed, and I closed my eyes.

It wasn't often that I won a battle with her.

She grabbed one of her shoes and hit me in the face.

It was a blow out of nowhere.

I was scared and angry.

I fell out of bed.

I remember raising my fist.

I remember its terrible weight in the air.

I remember Holly grabbing the wine bottle, smashing it against the wall.

Life is learned about in the movies, especially westerns.

I remembered my Mother.

I embraced Holly and she shook in my arms.

"You can't be a little boy forever," she protested. "A real man would have hit me back."

Holly was another photograph soon taken out of my wallet.

■ ■ ■

"You can't be a little boy forever," Joe said.

He insisted that I had to have breakfast in bed and the meal was so elaborate that I was actually gaining a little weight.

"What do you mean?" I asked.

"You gotta take this thing like a man. You need to do things, hijo."

I nodded, trying to look interested.

Joe took the orange juice from me, "I mean it. You shouldn't be ashamed."

"Like you in those Speedos? God, you're practically falling out."

He had been sunbathing on our roof. "Falling out. Falling in love. The fall of Rome. That's me."

I laughed because that made Joe a little less anxious.

The trick worked for he left quietly and quickly; I was safe, alone, in bed; I wasn't either dreaming or sleeping.

I was dying.

Was I dying?

This was Joe's house.

I had borrowed someone else's bed for my deathbed.

■ ■ ■

Actually I started to feel better again, mobile and spoiled.

Joe came home with a broken nose; gay bashing on DaVinci Street had become a popular tourist attraction.

I was terrified to touch him.

I was terrified of his blood.

It was my blood that was infected, but logic is illogical when it's most needed.

AIDS had been a storm under my skin, a series of high and low tides without a moon to explain its pattern.

Joe didn't need a neon sign to see where I was coming from.

Without a further word he left my bedroom.

I listened for signs of him in the house.

I called up Alice and Alberto but they weren't home.

I forced myself to find my friend.

Joe was in the kitchen, the room most like hell on this planet, the room where the body is fed and the soul is starved.

"Are you OK, José?"

"No, actually I'm not. I got a broken nose. I can't afford the bill from the emergency room. And I live with a ghost."

I felt dizzy so I sat down. "You asked me to move in with you. This is your fantasy."

I said this as if I was lawyer.

"I'm taking care of you because no one else can. Because no one else loves you."

I was almost an orphan, so close.

My Father had visited me once but when he learned I had AIDS he backed away.

I remember him backing out of the cul-de-sac during Mother's wake.

I was living in a home movie being played backwards, except that I was falling into the future.

José sat down next to me. "They all blame me you know. That I seduced you and that I gave you this disease."

"I did it all on my own," I said slowly. "Freud would have said that I picked the wrong woman because I only know how to live in a storm. And if I had picked you. Whew, me? Happy?"

Yes, José was right; friends and family were convinced that I had been gay all along.

If I had been gay I would have loved this man.

He was a good man.

A wave broke inside my head and came out of my body.

Before I knew it I was sitting in my own piss.

José got up and helped me to another chair.

He massaged my back. "Catch your breath, baby, and then we'll change you."

"Change me or my clothes?"

José tried to dismiss the whole thing, "It's OK. It's OK. We got a mop, no? It's OK."

But of course it wasn't.

■ ■ ■

"Mother pushed the chairs aside while I turned up the radio."

I paused in the story and José waited patiently, or was he humoring me?

"She put the radio real loud."

"Was it disco?" José wanted to know.

We were in his bed and he had his arms around me.

I felt safe, like I had found my own twin. "I don't remember."

"I'm going to pretend it's disco. Happy music. Remember happy music?"

"I'm sorry that you have to end up taking care of me," I said quietly.

I had been planning this moment for a long time.

I wanted to say that I loved him, my José, but instead I said, "That broken nose makes you look butch now."

"Now you like me."

"No, now I love you."

We sat there in silence and it wasn't like we were two lovers, not like two buddies in a foxhole.

I felt human.

"Go on," José said, "Tell me that story. I love fiction. Especially when it's based on real life. I don't know. It's philosophical but with a hint of entertainment, no?"

I had to speak slowly because each word cost me something (what?): "Mother pushed the chairs aside while I turned on the radio. We danced. I remember her laughing and laughing because I was so clumsy. Father came home and caught us dancing. He cut in and they really were good together. She followed my father's lead and then she would do something to try to trip him up."

"Where were you all this time?"

"I was leaning against the sink."

"That's a great memory," José said. "Imagine some people are so happy that they have a disco right in their kitchen."

"That was the calm before a storm, storms," I said without a trace of bitterness.

"Ssssh," he said with a firm voice, "Keep a good memory good."

"Like this one?"

He nodded and we sat there in silence.

I would die soon, soon enough.

I have been a happy man.

Few will believe it so.

José kissed me on the forehead and went downstairs.

I listened to him doing the dishes, singing along with the radio.

How did the two of us end up so unloved when we deserve the great and sacred burning heart of Jesus, his apostles, and all the other secret hosts of heaven?

Blood Never Rusts: A Novella in Verse

1.

Jorge shaves for a gigante Saturday night

What's a secret matador like me doing
working in a factory with men the color
of unbaked bread? My new job is
ancient. My calluses are fortunetellers.
Last night, in the Santería chat room,
I was warned of Sodom's paychecks, but
doesn't El Papa over there in gray Rome
have better things to do with his holy frown
than spy on me sweating because of a real
man and not work? My Christian name is
good at the spent currency exchange on
Detroit and Monroe: currency or what's
current? My sex life is life, aches as
claims: *this* world, *my* dance music, *my* bones.
Jorge, amigos call me, but I am a mystery.

2.

Leo in the locker room welcomes Jorge to hell

Remind me: is this the end or start
of my shift? Hey, Guitar Gus and
Ash are hooking up at *Mugshots*.
Jorge—isn't it? Join us. Or not.
Your Aztec ass must be worn out
like mine. Nakedness at work turns us
into interchangeable cogs.
This scar came from an angel's claw.
Suit yourself. Ignore me, but someday

you'll be old too. But I've a cold one
waiting for me. Heaven is a dry
county, so I've heard. I fish, Jorge,
because it's the only part of
the Bible that makes sense: sharks
and dolphin didn't freeload on
Noah's ark. I'm told we still have
gills in our throats. Odd to eat old gods.
You're crazy, working out after work.

3.

Jorge and Leo turn happy hour at Mugshots into a tradition

Baseball taught me to be Latino, Leo:
One mile away from Wrigley Field
was our Puerto Rico reigned by
Roberto Clemente. Fathers would
press their sons' faces into the blue
face of fame and say, "*Allí*, against
the odds, a Latino on the loose."
I hated playing baseball because
the family speculated about
their retirement on my slow fast ball.
The cousins hated the one of us
who'd hit the home run, the one of us
who was given a taste of rum while
the rest of us drank up sweat.
When that plane was swallowed
by the sea and Roberto became
a statue, Father told me that his
dream was to play the pros but
then I came along and he became

another ghost at the factory.
To this day when I hear a player
being interviewed and he has
a Spanish accent, I think of
my father and thousands of
his brothers shaping generations
so that a ball flying out of the park
looks a falling star in reverse.

4.

Ash warns Leo in the Target parking lot

You and Jorge, buddy, too two
peas in the wrong pod—comprende?
Men have been talking. That you're
taking it up the Alamo. See this black
eye? Would Zorro kick ass for you?
He's from the wrong side of the tracks, border.
We grew up together and rode sticks
called Trigger; John Wayned-it in gym;
bare knuckled it to be kings of school.
So I tell you: white is white and that's
how it is. The gene pool is a genius.
Jorge eats black beans while we're safe
building mansions of white bread.
Jorge's paycheck is just money and
doesn't have the magic to change his color.
You and me—we're the color of ghosts.
Like it or not, the moon's our mirror.
Are you two friends or are you amigos?

5.

Jorge and Leo laugh in a parked car in downtown Toledo

JORGE:

Workers share the shine of sweat.
Adam, Cain and Chicken George were
condemned to work by the sweat
of their brows. That's God's worst
punishment, the stealing of time.
Is it a plan to divide and conquer?
I don't believe that the blind stars
give a damn about strange apes looking
at their fate lines for road directions.

SKINHEAD WITH A CROWBAR:

Look! A Mexican jumping bean
and his ugly boyfriend! Laughing
and grabbing America by the balls!
We, the impure, know purity.
We know skulls break like eggshells.
We know blood can polish our boots.

LEO:

This isn't a dream. I'm not a dreamer.
The American dream is more of a flop
house than a skyscraper. Babylon, we've
sheltered your politicians. I'm screaming:
the dictionary can't explain these dicks.
I'm all voice, a useless fire alarm in Hell.

JORGE:

He's not my lover. Leave him alone, por favor.
What will his wife think when neighbors
wink? An iceberg turned the Titanic into

a soap opera, but you don't have that power.
Señor Faggot, to you. You're amateur
bill collectors, arguments for The Pill.
You want me to suck your New World?
Fake conquistadors! Eternal virgins!
Pobrecitos, you'll never receive love letters.

6.

Jorge refuses to pray in Saint Vincent Hospital

Leave the weak TV on, gracias.
I think that commercials are
the true art form of this age:
dancing furniture (chairs
that look like harps but that
also waltz together), cars with
Midwest accents (but not as
nasal as those in Wisconsin),
shoes, jeans, computers, and
there's even a seat for me
at the Crystal Cathedral, achoo,
amen. I sit and sit. My body
is used to working so I find
it strange to be a lazy Kennedy
as my wounds take stage center.
See these cards? From strangers
who say they love me because
I bled in their—*our*—city. White
hate gets embarrassed being
in bare ass. Under these bandages
I'm the Invisible Man, bad Hollywood.

I've been making statements all day
but, tragically, the police don't
want poetry. My union sent flowers—
because I'm gay? I prefer that mechanic
on the swing shift, someone loved
by God. The news is making big bucks
out of showing my face across Ohio.
I want a share in the ratings, that anti-reality.
Por favor, smuggle me a blank notebook.

7.

Andrew Carnegie in Heaven proves he knows the Earth

LIBERAL PUBLISHERS:
Shit, Jorge is a writer! If I (really) wanted
a Latino writer, I'd choose someone more
awkward with English, a houseboy with charm.
Foreigners shouldn't pass as one of us.
Also, books shouldn't stink of abstract sweat.
At least porno doesn't demand good grammar.

ANDREW CARNEGIE:
Publishers, why be passive aggressive just
to end up a poor bastard—unlike me? Steal big.
Be a giant petty crook. Tell you what—
publish one spick, and praise him to make
the other beaners write just like him and
then publish one more just to prove lightning
can strike twice, without end. And then
never publish another Columbus again.
But get grants for development, searches,
training, reprints. Look at me. Libraries

were built on blood (not mine), grand gestures
to workers who didn't deserve the right
to read. Most were foreigners. Most were men
trying to fuck just to pop babies to someday
conquer the vote. They believed democracy
existed! The shitheads voted for shadow men
who hocked their family jewels for my knuckles.
The masses now praise my libraries—get it?

8.

Leo drinks beer in his backyard and feels as old as the Earth

If I ever retire, I will polish
the pennies that no one picks up.
I've been wondering if each explosion
in deep space is a candle God
has blown out. How tired He must be
making wish after wish, wearing
the darkness after the lit cakes.
My dog is named Paris, he who
cannot save this muddy backyard
from the past of his slow tracks.
His war is with wings in the garden.
Paris is my wife's shadow for
he senses I don't need his protection.
That's sad. I never have left Toledo,
never had to. There isn't much time
after work to map the actual world.
My wife Ruthie is right to say wrongs
seem to have box seats without
ever paying for them. Jorge is healing.
Might as well live where you'll die.
Paris, show me your teeth's diamonds!

9.

Singing and dancing honest working men

WORKERS IN ONE VOICE:
Work, work, work
Until you're empty
As your pockets
Help the undertakers
Retire on your blood
You'll work in purgatory

WORKER #1:
It wasn't always like this.

WORKER #2:
Oh, yes it was.

WORKER #3:
I wanted a red sports car.

WORKER #4:
A broken condom.

WORKER #5:
Sick parents.

WORKER #6:
I hated books.

WORKER #7:
An honest dollar, huh.

WORKER #1:
I wanted to be a rock star:
I'm not a nice boy anymore
It's boring living next door
I'm trading my badges in for vice
I want to become black ice

10.

Ruthie hangs laundry on a foggy day

Do they eat tuna casseroles in Puerto Rico?
Am I always Leo's wife—even on a map
with countries named Unknown, Uncharted, Blank?
When Mr. Ross's son drowned, we were told
that the Maumee River was evil, that
its big blue mouth could eat any of us
without feeling guilty. Mother told us
of her childhood's sea, how drowned men
were dragged into fishing nets, how their eyes
had turned the blue of old glaciers. This all
confused me for this wasn't the sea that we
read about in books with pictures of golden
lighthouses, sailors with pipes and seagulls
singing to whales that were breathing like
geysers. It's possible to drown on land.

11.

Jorge returns to work and accepts Ash's apology during a break

There are hurricanes without
water or winds that can still
change the view or one's life.
While making coffee, for example,
the world can change to mud.
Or one can swim in landlocked
nights, complex simple embraces.
And my family Bible is full of sex
that doesn't feel too ancient.
I've learned desire needs us too,
that Lot's wife chose to honor

that city of symmetrical lovers.
Weekends yield to the yes of work.
My paycheck is not supposed
to be my autobiography.
It mistakes sweat for tears.

12.

After praising Ruth's mock key lime pie, Jorge gets drunk and explains why he is afraid of going to a gay bar tonight

At 13, I worked in a factory instead
of playing tennis with other niños.
Oil left me looking the rabid raccoon,
old black mask of labor. The music
piped in had the occasional mad polka
and opaque workers would pretend
to dance with each other and I'd hum.
My public paycheck went to the family,
but I'd whine for the Hardy Boys' latest
adventure as white sons of a lawyer.
I was an illegal screw threader and worked
before school and right after it. *Worked.*
I was once invited to go for root beer floats
but I had to put butter—if not bread—
on the family table. There are many Americas
never to be mine. Do you know that clocks
don't exist in bars? A cock can be a passport
to that place where language is unneeded.
Sodom is full of throbbing music, cult
followers of disco. It's smoke and mirrors
taking some R & R, a bed too crowded with
ghosts. I don't like how sweaty I get loving

clubs that tremble with the terrible heartbeats
of an army of lovers seeking exhaustion.
And something gets loose from me—prayers?
I leash a volcano, baby talk to the moon.
Frailty, I have no forwarding address.
Destiny, you will yet pay for my taxi.
Tight pants and all, I am future imperfect,
and soon, it's last call, a return to mortality.

13.

Sunday morning and Jorge isn't alone

Am I Latino, gay, union member, tax payer, sinner?
Yes, sí, I hope so. You turn my bed blue with human
breaths. Don't tell my foreman, my pretend father, but
I'm calling in sick tomorrow, because you must stay
here, and why pay off debts when I can bring gifts
to my impatient diary? De verdad, Marx was wrong
to romanticize the worker, wrong not to know
that erections can also be questions, wrong
not to unpack tenderness the way he did tender.

14.

Jorge hangs out in the hood because he feels lost

I just came for the drive, but amigos seek
saviors in their own image. Feed on
stock market crumbs, hermanos. Religion
and hormones compete without
endorsement deals, without sweeps
weeks. Let's go, they say, let's burn
without mourners, drink jukeboxes,

and praise the blurring that is its own
blessing. Drive faster, says Antonio,
and play louder and longer runes of
tunes. We don't want to stop too often,
just for drive-through expressionless beer.
The moon takes photographs of us that
it forgets to ever share. Hombres, we don't
stop being targets just by driving in circles.

15.

Leo and Jorge go fishing

LEO:
I'm retired and you're fired. Not fair,
but there it is. There, you heard it from
my mouth. Worms, hooks, river . . . time.
They fired you for existing. It wasn't
because you were late once too often.
They watched the clock, their private spy.
The factories are rusting all around us.

JORGE:
Blood never rusts. It becomes history.
The gene pool has libraries, but not
like those reigned in by Franklin. Blood
is designed to be real red so to be read
easily. The past is a naked guide.

LEO:
Remember? We were talking of stupid
things—like how ice is for sale
at gas stations? Ice is the opposite
of motion. It made sense then.
Then glass, a mass of glass, loss.

JORGE:
Fast fists. They took my pants down,
to prove that I wasn't bigger or better.
They had watched too many films called
Latin Heat, South of My Border, or *A Gringo's*
Souvenirs. I wore their spit like a cheap
wedding dress. Then words, curses, one man
pissed on me, *hey Golden Boy, King Midas's*
Pig. I was explicit before Satan. And then
the cutting, the rhetorical questions, blackness.
I've scars never to become monuments.

LEO:
This is now. The fish are as shy as the *Book*
of Revelation. It hints, never tells, just gossips.

JORGE:
We don't need nest eggs, Leo—we've optimism.
We all work towards salvation, work like dogs
until we're dog-eared, doggerel, dogma.
I will never be a rock star, a rock of ages, but
I will write. Of this, the blood, the red years
of rum and coke, the hunger for jalapeños
when it was whispers I wanted in my mouths,
my red Ohio. I will write of the fish too wise
to be eaten by us and of the evilness of keeping
amigos like us apart, of how men affect my
facts, of the profound shit that will be my job
to turn into gold. I'll be proud to go through
the needle's eye without a stitch of clothing.

X, My EX

I met a Zorro of my own at one of those rooftop barbecues Chicago is famous for, where tenants bring out their potted plants and create green walls between the party and the city.

These provide convenient urban vomitoriums over alleyways already over-stimulated with banana peels; broken bottles of beer; dog shit; used (incredibly stretched) condoms; store-bought tomato sauces used by men whose mothers never taught them to cook or else they who have careers that demand more time than is theirs to give; boots left by mysteriously barefooted men; chopped green onions too strong for someone's aging stomach. The frightening smell of alcohol-inspired vomit is never really noticed.

I was still in my writer's phase, wearing carefully black glasses, tight button-down jeans, a loose white shirt with a generous V-neck that exposed my chest, deck shoes that never did taste salt water, and a gold earring chosen because of the way it flared against my tanned ear, like I was the grandson of some pirate. My Caribbean, unfortunately, was nothing very exciting except when my blood would stir.

I had run into Quentin on Addison Street; he was throwing a farewell party for himself, before he went "to Rome to act like a Greek."

"Emir, you're much too tanned. That means that you're getting up early in the morning. It means there is no one in your bed pulling you back into it. It means you have to come to my party and meet someone. A word to the wise. When I look for a lover, I always choose the palest boy in the bar."

I had been trying to convince myself that I could handle being alone for a very long time and so I surprised myself by showing up at the party. I had stopped having a sex life ever since all my blood stayed in my brooding head.

The fiesta was as boring as I had expected it to be—until a man in a Zorro costume walked in. Everyone at the party was a little too cool to stay surprised for more than seconds. They quickly avoided looking directly at the stranger hesitating by the door. Amused, I walked over to introduce myself but Quentin was already there: "And who might this tall but dangerously dark stranger be?"

A man without love has the best hunter instincts, even if that man is Quentin.

Zorro mumbled something. A blonde man stepped from behind him; it was Jerry, a nice man known for cruising the johns at Wrigley Field whenever the Cubs were losing, or in other words, often. Jerry's theory was that straight men need to feel like barbarian conquerors, even if just by breaking the law in a losing team's bathrooms. "This is my new neighbor," he purred.

I nodded to both of them.

Jerry continued, "He's from Utah. I told him that costumes were acceptable and he thought I said it was a real costume party. I wanted to see everyone's face!"

I joined in the laughter at first, but became annoyed at Jerry's condescension to his own date. I was also disappointed that Zorro was yet another white man trying to imitate a Latin lover. Sometimes I felt like I was on the road touring with *West Side Story*. "Do you know what's so funny?" I asked.

"No, I must say I don't actually," Zorro replied in a very gentle voice.

"In Chicago, some people call any man's drag outfit a costume. So, this costume party is a make-yourself-at-home-affair."

He looked around to confirm the fact that he was the only one wearing a mask. Others were dressed in drag, as not themselves, or as themselves far from yearbook photographers. Zorro finally said, "Well the damage is done. And anyway no one will know who I am or what I look like as long as I keep my mask on."

I patted him on the back. "Jerry, this man deserves a drink. I'll return him to you as soon as I toast him."

Before Jerry could protest, I pushed Zorro towards the improvised bar of six crates topped by a redwood plank which was covered by someone's spare Italian tablecloth.

"What do you drink?"

"Vodka."

"And?"

"Vodka and everything else," Zorro laughed.

I smiled.

"Emir is your personal bartender and I pour you some vodka and tonic. I'll even slip in some moonlight too . . . unless tonight's hero is allergic to moonlight?"

His smile brought back a memory of breaking a mirror one drunken morning in San Juan. How astonished I was to see the sun burning in each piece of glass even as I leaned forward and could see myself from so many different angles. I felt translucent, beautiful, and that was exactly how X made me feel—at first, at least at that first meeting.

I smiled right back. "So let's introduce ourselves. What's your name?"

He paused and told me it was __________, but I was sure he had given me a fake name in case I ever tried blackmailing him or something. I asked for his wallet. It was a traditional black leather wallet, with a few plastic frames for pictures and credit cards. His driver's license had an old picture of him, wearing a young man's silly but serious mustache, his hair parted in the middle, his shoulders softer, rounder in a red and black shirt instead of that cape he was wearing.

"So __________ is your real name," I laughed.

He shrugged, "A personal life has to have a few facts, no?"

"I'll call you X. My life needs a little mystery." Then I added with a stare, "Although I prefer a big mystery."

We ended up sneaking out of there; he threw his mask away; I flagged a taxi; X stayed overnight; we were two slippery bastards trying to hold on to each other for as long as we could.

It was as simple and as complex as that.

The next morning he told me he had never slept with a man before. I was both flattered and frustrated because I knew, even then, that no one holds on to training wheels for very long. He stayed by my side for one year. I kept the calendar we bought together, *Naked Archaeologists*. I figured it would become a collector's item someday if my writing career ever takes off—¡Grand Hijo de Sputnik!—It was marked with appointments, birthdays, days to put out the recycle bins, reminders, dinner dates in which we would try to keep the romance alive and not just bounce our bones against each other in bed.

If not, maybe the calendar may give someone erections years after I'm dead.

Fuck you, X. Or I mean, don't fuck you. I don't know what I mean anymore.

■ ■ ■

Quentin's last words to me, before he went on yet another pilgrimage to Rome, were, "Emir, don't be a smartass and act like all your blood is in between your legs. One man gone just means there is one more man to be found."

Maybe it was good advice—I don't know—but my ex-lover always treated me as if I lived in a world that was larger than my bed.

It used to be our bed.

Maybe I'm a little old-fashioned, but I was happy with X—me Tarzan, you Tarzan. I am a Puertorriqueño and I love one thing about me—how I carry things to extremes. Some people accuse me of being "Latino Cool" but I think of the word "hip" which right now makes me think of my ex's hands slowly turning my body to face him, we're at the Century Mall, we're riding up the glass elevator to the fourth floor to buy a new lamp for the apartment, we kiss each other, I'm dizzy from the kiss, from turning away from the kiss and looking out the glass walls at a world growing smaller, and goddamn it, it still seems an important moment . . . .

I must think about something else as I ride past the Sears Tower in this taxi, late for a dinner. The tower as seen through the back of the taxi window is a haunting pillar. It's as if I'm expecting to see us still up there, black stick-figures looking through the telescope like tourists, searching for something so very far away, something that might makes us smile. How strange that I actually fell in love once and I was loved in return.

The taxi driver yells out, "Did you say something?"

"Get me the hell out of here. There's ice melting in a martini with my name on it."

The man smiles into the rear view mirror. "Now, there's a reason I can understand. I'll get you there in a flash."

And he does, minutes later I'm there. Where am I and is this my life? I step out on unsteady feet, a little carsick, perhaps a little what my grandmother used to call "heartsick."

I tip the driver well and he motions me closer. He looks around, as if about to share a secret. "Do you know why taxi drivers are the best lovers?"

I shrug.

"Taxi drivers are the best lovers because they know how to stick it to you."

I smile on cue. "I don't kiss on the first date."

The man reveals a broken smile, "It's not your hand I want to hold."

I wave him on, he blows me a kiss, and I then walk into the brownstone where the dinner party is starting late right on time. It's an ordinary affair and so I can be a robot about it. I'm not even sure what we're celebrating, or even if, we are celebrating anything.

I wonder what X is doing right now. I'm tired of always feeling as if I'm waiting for something, or for someone to catch up with me.

■ ■ ■

The phone is ringing as I walk in. God, don't salesmen or telemarketers have private lives? "Hello?"

"It's Linc. Emir, are you sitting down?"

I clear my throat. "Is this an obscene call by an amateur?"

"No listen, seriously. I saw him. *Him*."

"Who?"

"X!"

"Where the hell did you see him?" I gasp.

"By the Belmont Rocks. I thought he was supposed to be in Cowboy Heaven looking for a cowgirl of his own?"

"Are you sure it was him?"

Linc growls, "I slept with him too, you know."

"Who didn't?" I answer, hands shaking while reaching for a drink, a pen to play with, something to hold on to.

"What are you going to do?"

"About what, Linc?"

"That he's back in town."

"Linc, what can I do? Get a posse together and run him out of town? Nobody tar-and-feathers anymore. Another lost American art form."

I swallow the drink. It's vodka from last night. It's warm. It's hot. I'm on fire. I'm Dante without a handsome firemen in whose arms I can faint. I want to throw up.

"Get off your bullfighting ass and come over. I'll buy some wine and you can cry all you want to in my waterbed."

Linc won't put up with me today. I don't want to go there; I don't want to be safe; I don't want to rent a video. I want to stay home in case X decides to come over. The bastard has probably abandoned the woman he abandoned me for. Maybe he has spent secret nights looking at our photographs from sojourns in sunlight. Puerto Rico feels so much a dream that perhaps it can only be inhabited by dreamers.

"If you don't come over, I'll come over there and kidnap you. I'm not putting up with this shit anymore. I'm tired of its stink."

Linc is yelling so loudly that I have to pull the phone away from my ear.

"Can you pick me up?" I ask him slowly.

"About time you ask me that! Give me ten minutes."

Linc slams the phone down and I slowly put mine down, as if it's fragile and might break any second. My heart is beating so fast. I feel like my heart is going to burst. The stupid piñata isn't going to last all night long. My dick isn't a stick; it's just a dick; it's just a dick. My heart is so crowded and it feels especially tiny today.

■ ■ ■

Linc is asleep and I'm jealous of his talents as a corpse. I write this without turning any lights on, thrilled at the sense of danger: my pen slipping off the college-ruled lines. I enjoy the problem of being unable to read the last word that leads to this word and this word and this word. I love surprising myself. How dangerous to dream without sleeping and one moment in *One Day in the Life of Ivan* . . . a man cries because there are no stones in his soup. They alone prove he can taste things, the world as some physical reality. I dress the front window in the informal veil of my breath.

X isn't raging down the streets of Chicago. He isn't the Godzilla of love. A little disappointed, I look up into the night sky, connect the stars. A lot disappointed. Tonight I see a whale, a pale whale, in the cosmos. Whose whale is this that is beached in the black sky of 3:14 AM?

Poor John, my best friend from Milwaukee hung himself before seeing it. How he loved the ocean and its "living dinosaurs": "Moby Dick had the best press agent, that's all." When he was first diagnosed with AIDS he insisted that he was suffering from Darwin's Delight, destruction of the unfit. The newspapers claimed that John killed himself because he went temporarily insane as a side effect of experimental medications he had put himself on. His friends knew that his suicide was just like John in bed, in business, everywhere:

No, I'd rather do it myself. I've come to believe Job is the Bible's true hero, forever waiting for Justice to heal him with the very sword that cuts him.

I eventually fall asleep.

I wake up to Linc busy on a painting that looks like a bludgeoned rooster so I sneak out and take the bus back to Boystown. When I return to my apartment, the first thing that I do is check on the answering machine. Not one message. X didn't call me. God, I sound more and more like a drag queen in a Tennessee Williams play. X didn't call me. I need a Bloody Mary. Sin tastes a lovely red early in the morning. I open up the blinds and blinded by the light passing through the moon-spurned ice cubes disappearing without a sound in my drink.

Good morning, heartache, sit yourself down. Let's take turns telling war stories. Pity is one of the few luxuries that survivors claim for themselves.

X didn't call me.

▪▪▪

A week later, I find a note stuck under the carpet by my front door. It's from X. He had stopped by while I had been at my cousin Olivia's house. I wish I hadn't come home alone and that X had been waiting for me on the floor next to the door I painted blue one day when I was homesick for the sea. How lovely the fantasy of X catching me with someone named Lorenzo or Ramundo. Well maybe "caught" isn't the right word since this isn't the age of the great white hunter, is it?

The note says that he waits to meet me tomorrow at the Art Museum restaurant at noon because he has an important question for me. I stop reading. What am I going to do? I've lived long away from him to be independent or at least a little less clumsy about weekend nights. But I remember X oh so well.

How he valued his privacy. This became especially clear during the first time we went to Puerto Rico together. We had been sleeping naked in the private rock garden that was part of the cottage we had rented. Everything was green or blue. It was as if we were Adam and Steve. I was Adam because I named everything about us. I called our garden El Mundo, the world.

He woke me up: "Do you think you'll ever write about me?"

I laughed because I had been expecting some kind of bad news. "As soon as you do something interesting."

He stood up. "Promise me that you'll never use my name or call me by any name that people could guess who I am."

"You're not that important," I teased. "Most people don't know you even exist."

He turned away from me and I noticed that his bikini lines were starting to yield to the waves of Caribbean light breaking over his body. I can describe what he tasted like, what he felt like, what he gave me, but I'm unable to fairly describe his long legs, spacious chest, shy cock, strong back and hands that were always trembling.

"If you write about me I'll shoot myself right in the head."

"What the hell are you talking about? Look," I said, kneeling so that I could stare into his eyes, "I will write about you. You're one of the most important things in my life. But you don't have to worry. No one reads my work and the few that do don't know what the hell I'm writing about most of the time."

He cupped my face with his hands. "I can't go on with you if I think what I'm doing now is going to be shared with the rest of the world. Hell, I can't even sleep just in my underwear. Honey, I value my privacy."

"And I value your privates," I said sitting down on the cement floor.

He sat down next to me, "Just think of me as the invisible man. Write about someone else, that's all."

I sat up: "I told you a long time ago, the day we met actually, that I was going to call you just X!"

"X?"

"X!"

"X," he repeated.

"X as in the mysterious Mr. X."

He kissed my neck. "As in X marks the spot."

I kissed him back on the mouth. "As in X equals Y."

He pushed me away, but not too far away. "As in X-Con?"

I just fell back on the wet cement. "All right, let's get it out of our systems so we can concentrate on other things than the alphabet. X as in X-cellent, X-tra special, X-ternal, X-mas, X-tract . . ."

He interrupted, "As in X-communicate, X-lover, X-tra work, X-. . ."

"Stop it. Why pick out the sad words?"

He put his head on my chest. "Emir, I'm X-tra sensitive I guess."

"Stop it," I said, "I may not even write a book about Señor X. Not if he keeps me so busy that I won't have time to work on a book."

He did try to distract me for the rest of the vacation and we walked around with the halo of each other's kisses on our foreheads.

Since he left me, I've been X's real widower. Yes, sí, a man can be another man's widower.

I look away from the note he wrote me, a note flowering with a handwriting no longer glazing birthday cards. He has written more, but I need to pause before finishing his note. I need to know my own heart before I decided whether to meet him or not. Meet, meat.

OK, I'm ready for more. X, thanks for this séance on plain white paper.

"It may be a shock," X writes, "but I'm getting married. I want—no, I need you—to be there. She knows everything about you. I want to love you in this new and maybe strange way."

So many reactions at the same time.

Everything about you.

My best man.

Married.

Anger turns into embarrassment as I catch myself honestly feeling disappointed. At myself? At my tragedy dumbing down into soap opera? I start to laugh. It's a wild laugh, a laugh that's scaring me even as I sink into it; it's a punchline without a joke.

I've been playing Señor Secrets all this time when it's been so obvious to everyone but me: I can love. That being loved isn't like one of Superman's powers that show up just as he is being poisoned by Kryptonite. Salsa requires the adrenalin of the drum.

I take X's note, fold it into an airplane, release it into the air. I don't have to witness its crash.

The noon of the next day crawls to me. I picture X waiting for me among the sculptures, by the Picasso with bathers on an abstract beach. He too is a work of art, one that I molded under my breath, that I shaped with my legs and arms, and that I bronzed with my slow tongue. He will wait for me forever, or for at least an hour. I know him: X will track me down and I will eventually agree to the off-off-off-off-etc. Broadway wedding. Just because a love story is over doesn't mean that the lovers stop existing.

Let X sweat it out for a change.

Let X chase me, even if only as un amigo.

Let X work hard for his salvation.

It's my turn to be seduced. The letter X is nothing more than a man with his arms and legs spread open. It will never equal why.

THE MACHO DOLLS
Flash Fictions

Meet The Macho Dolls

We sing in salsa bars where a college ID gets you a free sex-on-the-beach or a Cuba Libre hangover. It's hard to compete with hormones, for harmony to be heard over bad rum. We're a boy band, hijos in the costumes of body hair and proud Adam's apples. Once, I stared at a matador who winked at me as if my diary was on eBay, page by page. I sang my heart out so the rest of me could follow.

■ ■ ■

I'm cast as the Big Brother, a tenor, near priest, bear among bulls, not Boy Wonder. Boy bands airbrush their beards, at first. Sure, I seek praise, even if it has a terrible retirement plan. I sang in the womb. I'm a Psalmist in tight jeans and with an agent hungrier than Spain was for gold. I'll sing with *The Macho Dolls* until I go solo, until my goatee is my glory and confession, until I go Hollywood, until I'm another tragic capitalistic son-of-a-bitch.

■ ■ ■

Our first single is "Dance Like the Devil That You Are." But the song tumbles to the hell saved for carnies. We're too toothy, too air brushed by caring parents, not yet telegenic enough for this age of youthful tears. Our dizzy spin doctors go into frenzy: "The band is Salomé with big balls, like low riders pounding on astronauts." Macho. Not Dolls. Off-the-charts, we are dead. They want to give us a new name: *Piñata Posse. The Border People.* No, gracias, thanks for nothing. Lawyers read clauses as if love letters from robber barons.

■ ■ ■

Meet *The Macho Dolls*: Raúl: red (everywhere), Buddhist cocksman, fisherman, man's man. Topher: a séance with muscles, uniform-addict, boy storm. Mockingbird: married (a great secret), book lover, heart thief. Luis: tattooed Boy Scout, dancing chess master, shy studio czar. Me, Manuel: flamenco diarist, midnight compass, Lorca's boy toy.

■ ■ ■

I offered a poem but it was jailed as an album cut. There are no longer "B sides" that might be played accidentally. No alphabet in our destiny. Not the B as in B movies, B in breathalyzer tests, B in the boy I am under my chaps and chattering tattoos, B as in genius balls. My poem will never become a single, never be promiscuous among stranger's ears in cars, planes, in secret motels. "Who wants to talk about God while sucking face?" But, I insist, semen is about prophesy.

■ ■ ■

A blind DJ in Tampa plays my song (por que?): "Blonde in Your Bed." It's a spark. Soon it burns like bad news, gossip too delicious to be true or false. Soon we must make a video. Soon it's made: everyone wears a wig. One by one we're naked, but without proof of the pudding, the big enchilada, the true arrow. We look like drunk unicorns who have a hit!

I am blonde in your bed
You are as dark as the dead
It's not the vodka in your head
I am blonde in your bed

■ ■ ■

We hit the #1 spot quickly on all of the music charts. At last, the abyss finds us sexy! All that glitters isn't a gold record. We hire a choreographer as the true tailor of our dreams, profit as prophet. I have the lowest number of shiny magazine covers. To fix that I give long interviews in my bathtub. *Remember*, hisses my publicist, *you've never read an entire book and you'd only suck dick if it was a matter of national security*. The closet is a jock that's the wrong size. Sí, I'm the doll in *The Macho Dolls*. Sure, of course: I won't spill the gravy train, won't tame the wild piñata in public, won't sexualize our harmony.

■ ■ ■

Adult bookstores are embassies of nations without power. I love being anonymous except when a blue film starts revealing who they think I am. Some songs are best when they have no lyrics. When I finally zip up, the simmering starts again. What human joy there is in anticipation. I'm only offstage when anonymous in dark places where men never look at your face. Then, it's back to the tour where I sing of love, purgatory's poster boy.

Cuko Gets Nostalgic for Confusion

The mortician's only son's part-time job was to dress in a suit, sit in the mock chapel and weep loudly for strangers. I didn't believe they were real tears so once he wiped some on my lips. Saltier than the Great Salt Lake's name. Tato never complained about the tight suit, the Windsor knot, his sleeping ass, the stink of flowers only sometimes overpowered by the corpse-of-the-hour. He'd only really talked when we skinny-dipped at the quarry, when the clothes of grieving were off. He'd glow after swimming and we'd sleep under the sailor's sun to bleach our black hair to look like taco-stand surfers. Hikers sometimes called us faggots, butterflies, the rearguard, and we did kiss once: but nothing. So we put on hold our plan to run away to New York and wear leather to galleries. Now Tato is a greedy mortician and I'm just another soul in cyberspace. This CyberRaza loco, QueerVato, Hypertext sex addict drowns in memories of swimming in my young body that did its best to remain real. When Tato looks at me these days, he just sees a profit.

Lalo Tells of a Lost Weekend After Too Much Saki

Bruce is naked in the buzzing car and I'm fucking driving out of state, just like that. Break the gates at the toll booth. To the beach with its imaginary starfish? To the forest with unblessed eyes? Someplace where there is no noise or it's all natural noise. I'm loco, but why not dream big? He is my Bruce—for this week at last. And it feels good to have your humming man next to you while your red car throbs in the all-American night. Oh, yes, I forgot to tell you—that it's dark, but it's the summer so there's no need to shake unless you're trembling thinking about Bruce and me blurring on the unfolding highway. Not Bruce like in Springsteen—who must look sexy when you clean that frowning rocker up. Bruce, but not like in Bruce Willis, although I wouldn't kick him out of my junta. I know I will recognize the exit to get off just by the poetry of its name. It's not as simple as Paradise Alley or as sweet as Sodom Road. When is anything ever free in this country? Bruce has his head back and wears a handsome beard of wind. We have half a tank of gas left to spend as we survey our kingdom of fever.

Lucky, the Latin Lover of Lombard, Illinois

I slept with white lovers in the cul-de-sac suburbs who in the end just wanted me to say, "Caramba, Lucy" or "de plane, de plane." No zoot suit for this rico suave English major who claimed Sal Mineo's tragedy in *Rebel Without a Cause* as private property. *Home* was an island of smells: sofrito, carne asada, "Spanish" rice. We learned to love French fries, Boston baked beans, Buffalo wings. In the locker room at the pool, men praised my "full" tan but to me they were just ghosts in steam. Dressed, I was a spy among the mall people. I ironed my hair as friends permed theirs. The timing, it's about time. I had to take a foreign language class but I said I was already in honors English. I never dreamt of the wild west, or of mountain farms in Puerto Rico, but of the red city burning only miles from me. I'd take trains and disappear only to reappear in the suburbs as a messenger: *innocence isn't forever, amigos*. Our bodies were the wrong bridges of escape and so we drove up and down Main Street as if the dizzy sperm of astronauts circling the familiarized planet. One by one, I would always drop off my friends at their inevitably white-colored homes. Finally, when alone, as a ritual between the road and me, I'd blast *Black Magic Woman*. Sometimes I would cruise around, wave at the transvestites hiding off the Lilac Trail. For my 25th Class Reunion I was reported as "missing." So typical—as if their reality is the only one. I wasn't missing at all or how else could you find me in your bed tonight?

Pablito Goes Butch

There is a release from reality while bathing in a lake, the blur of bluing body parts in sky-fed water. We sit on the beach and as naked as the horizon; friends can often talk of nothing as the everything it is: "I thought life was going to tell me what it wants." "Like in sex?" "Yeah, kind of." "Oh, well." Then glowing beers are culled from the cold waters; laughter keeps us anchored to the night, *this* night.

■ ■ ■

We wake up in the latest fashion wear designed by bored mosquitoes. The woods are as unshaven as we are. "Too Hemingway," I mutter but I forget others only read their lifelines. Pissing into the sky, I'm sure I've never seen that cloud before, that it doesn't need my imagination. A crash of rain, a rush into the opaque tent, rum for breakfast, rock & roll lip-synch restlessness. "The fish won't forget their fates." Friends look at each other, shrug, itch. I disguise a story from *The Iliad* as gossip.

■ ■ ■

Bill calls himself "Bear" these days. Jeff's wife sleeps with a mechanic, but how their Jeep purrs. Lester prefers trees over humans, "Well, we stink like a bad rhyme." Our troubles came here with us for we are our troubles. I sit in the body of my silence and listen to winds in the trees, rivers that can't seem to answer our thirsts.

■ ■ ■

"I'm gay," says Bill and he's shocked that we know, have suspected it, have refused to leave him behind on the battle field (what war?). Lester wants details, but we're still too sober to gut the moon. When we're drunk from the cold river beers, the Supreme Court of Sperm decides: jacking off or getting a blowjob isn't gay. Kissing a man is the line in the sand, Judas's theme park.

■ ■ ■

Packing up, last photos, quick prowls through green paths, then the slow return. The burning highway, sunset as messenger: home in the dark, but I walk through my house as if a blind man who doesn't trip over his furniture. Nothing has changed. Mail is determined to make the word the real world. We won't call each other for weeks, not until the camping becomes stories. I sit on my bed and wonder why we dream at all when we have all this, then my doorbell does its two-note opera. I open the door for Bill and we don't have to exchange a word. I've waited years to be known by him. I kiss him back. He likes my morning beard, rawness without apology.

Los Tres Gatos Community Theater Presents Tennessee Williams' *Glass Menagerie*

Diego auditions with a speech from Prospero. He replaces one magic book with a first edition of Einstein's *Theory of Relativity*. Diego gets the theater to fall into a New Testament hush. The other actors envy Diego's fake-blonde beauty which allows him to goof. He bows and is back with me backstage. "Great" say a chorus of truck drivers and lawyers who scratch off one leading role from their wish list. Their Diego is no longer just their mailman, goddammit. It'll be my turn soon. "Do the hunchback chiropractor." But I've worked on something new, as I explain to the drunk director in the expanding theater. "I'm a heroin addict trying to decide if my blind date has a wooden leg or if it's just me." The expected giggles don't exist so I rush through my throat's orchestra, bow. Run off, off. I join a parade of pacers. Diego hits me on the back, sweet liar. Call backs: Diego. And ME! Happy hour at *Cactus José's* will be happy. For hours.

■ ■ ■

Darla calls all week but I won't go to Hawking Mall for new black clothes so that they have time to look old, housebroken, Valentino's hand-me-downs. She is trying to bed Diego by using me as a short-cut. I'm no toll bridge's troll. "Besides, no personal calls at work," I scream as Mr. Krakow calypsos by. This is our cue: call back in ten. I return to typing. Why black? Actors, by our nature, are mysterious without props. Well maybe not at last call, but who is?

■ ■ ■

The director asks Diego and me to stay. Wearing the dirty haloes of rivalry, we're handsome on that bare stage. "I'm in trouble," says Sid, short for Sidney or Siddhartha. "One of you is Tom and the other is The Gentleman Caller. But who is who?" "I'd like to be Tom," grins Diego just like Robert Redford in *The Way We Were*, "he's a heartbreaker." I shrug, "Just put Diego in underwear and let him smoke a cigarette in a St. Louis midnight. You'll sell out each night." It's decided. I'm Tom, more poetic. We're left alone in the theater and Diego offers a handshake, "You bastard and you are one clumsy martyr." He is happy for us, although it's not much of a challenge for him to be a handsome eclipse of a guest. I'm a petrified forest deserted by songbirds. Me—as Tom, the playwright's stand-in, the poet stuck in a St. Louis warehouse, the betrayer. I've only been a supporting actor in other plays (or as Diego has said, "everyone's jock"). I tried out just to get drunk and complain. I now understand Joan of Arc as comedian.

■ ■ ■

There are tricks in memorizing one's lines. Associate. Key words. Cues. Hypnotism. But soon Darla knows my role better than I do. Can one get stage fright before there's a stage? Rehearsals are terrible, hell. Diego's prompts anger the director and poor upstaged Laura is anything but fragile as she curses me for keeping the cast late. "Your bed needs a rest anyway," I snap back, but I'm not Tennessee Williams. Soon, the words come to me—words that feel mine, act as if mine. I'm Tom, the pissed-upon who wants to see the world naked at last. He gets lost in dark parks, and he is someone who isn't brave enough to become a stripper for bachelorette parties or gay men's flesh circuses. The blind voyeur. He writes poetry when not touching himself, hungover or eying an eyeful. He is in love with Diego the gentleman (landowner, almost?) and has only the sliver of a sister as a lure. Diego, the mysterious optimist, blonde Adam bomb, glowing Genesis bad boy, gentle man. Tom is Laura's rival—how Biblical, cosmic, dishonest, cutthroat. Actors find sore spots in their souls. Rub them. Rub them again. Rub them.

■ ■ ■

It's opening night and Diego and I drink blue gin in our dressing room. It's so small that we have no choice but to kiss. Are we acting? Soon, I'll be in costumes and makeup. Soon, the role will end. Soon, may very well be back to square one. Not yet. Broadway has us both by our short hairs. Diego and I hold on to each other before curtain time, before we're ghosts with cues, before applause simplifies this whetstone and sparks, before we please with masks on.

Sammy Sanchez, Country Singer

The high school gym is packed with boys in black nail polish and girls in Polka beauty. They pretend to know my lyrics. They just want to move their beautiful mouths.

■ ■ ■

It's a good set at Bubba's Buddha, speakeasy without the need to speak. Nice Tex-Mex, says a legal-age cowboy. Why does the *Book of Revelation* crow when we have less mysterious dangers? Am I a country or nation singer? Good luck on your Sombrero tour, the hunky one-man rodeo growls as he leans against me. His cowboy hat fails to hide the wildfire in his eyes. Sí, the Sombrero tour. ¡Gracias! This is officially now the Sombrero Tour. I know how to steal when I'm hungry. Cowboy, let's show God our bared heads.

■ ■ ■

The next gig is so small that there isn't a hotel anywhere near. We sleep under the stars, bathe in tequila bottles. Children knock on our van's windows: ¿tienen hambre? Sí, I've been starving most of my long life (even though I'm just 22 years old). We follow them across muddy meadows to a tin shack without saying a word to each other: this is magic! and we're awake and sober! We get fed homemade tamales and rice, the first taste of communion in weeks. It's a humble family's gift to strangers they think are poorer than they are. Our Samaritans offer us the perfect dessert; they pick up acoustic guitars, drums made out of coffee cans, and maracas full of pumpkin seeds. It's our time to listen. No—to hear.

■ ■ ■

We shower at a truck stop. We look like an immoral Trojan condom commercial. Even the roadies aren't carrying tomorrow's weight. There is horseplay until we feel like ponies again. Dressed, we are suddenly homesick. The fig leaf is an underappreciated gift from God. On stage, in my designed tight jeans, it looks like I've a frontier to offer.

■ ■ ■

Several labels circle and sniff us. Now that we are the largest majority of the minority, I have to sound more white than ever: power never selects an heir it thinks a bastard. I wear tighter pants and a looser voice. *I dedicate this to the red, white and blue girls and boys who love apple pie and guns and the tequila inside my illegal kisses.* The crowd goes loco and they stink of dinero and dueñe.

■ ■ ■

At a party (I thought maybe an orgy, but no!), a young Latino scholar almost spits in my face: why country music? you like gringos? Why, sí, I do. And they will bust your brown ass no matter the degree stuck up it. We're pulled apart, but later he wants to get high with me. He was just trying not to sound like a groupie so I would sleep with him: reverse seduction. I told him that I didn't want a career in a Mariachi band in a tourist restaurant famous for the size of their Margarita glasses. We drove around in his convertible and sang to each damn song on the radio, no matter the color of the voice. It took awhile for us to end up by a lake and stripped of ideas. Rest is one of the underpraised gods.

■ ■ ■

I sing "Stand By Your Man" in a Beaver, Pennsylvania Christian karaoke bar and I'm booed off the stage. The country roads, livestock and I brainstorm about how to win America's hearts and minds without me becoming a snack for conservatives. I need a hit record for dancers. When people dance, something in them is loosened: pocket change, hotel room keys, souls, or wishes they made to falling stars that never seem to set fields on fire.

▪ ▪ ▪

I'm under him when I suddenly spot his cop's uniform hanging on the closet doorknob. Shit, how did I get here? He thinks I'm a gardener because I wanted to be anyone but Sammy tonight. He follows my stare and kisses me slowly. Hey, hermano, I only use my handcuffs for work. I think I'm in Florida or Georgia—somewhere with grits served at breakfasts. He is trembling as I trace the constellation he might be if he is ever thrown into the sky. Sometimes it good to be afraid of yourself.

▪ ▪ ▪

We try on different band names: Montezuma's Revenge, Aztec Cowboys, The Legals. No, it's Sammy Sanchez. There can be an exception for one soul, not an entire tribe. Radios will soon sell my voice's mugshot. Only God enjoys being anonymous forever. In the van, I practice my autographing skills. Two capital letters and several wavy lines. Just get the date right, fucking idiota, says one of the guitarists, because you're just a diary entry to them. Or the one who gave them a social disease, adds the drummer. I ignore them and write my name over and over and over again. This is who I am now, I chant as if suddenly remembering a Buddhist meditation from several past lives ago, this is who I am now: S— S——.

Posing for Pablo

I've changed my name from Octavio: *call me Jude* I said, *sí, the Obscure*. I'm naked at this time, posing for Pablo, a trained artist while friends rummage through his bowls of apples. *Jude, come back to Earth*! Why is it called an art opening? Can it open its body, heart, bank account, legs, mind? Pablo growls: *Be a little more Samson-like or you'll fuck up my career.* Lowell is juggling Tony's comet earrings. Belinda breastfeeds a black book. Art, as a process, is slow, but mean like a volcano's itch. I mustn't look bored for I'm no overexposed Mona Lisa. It's a buzz to have a handsome painter's eye on you, that angry horse racing towards you, his mind opening you. *Jude*, I said, to my mother, and that was that. Giving myself birth seems extravagant, but no taxing this theater. Belinda opens the door for Jorge, he's back. I nod, he takes off his shirt and drinks beer in the fire escape. We do not love details enough, those tiny prophets. Weird to be so Post-Raphaelite this late in the game. I've always loved the expression: *he wouldn't know the truth if it bit him in the ass*. So American, and true. *Jude, more armpit, someone get him a beer, a lover*. Pablo is too old to be a young Turk. I'm bleeding again: a steak knife accident. I must think about blood, rubies. The red in Karl Appel's oeuvre, the red in the word *read*, the red mouths of the mummies of my coloring books. Crayons used by John-John Kennedy just went on auction, faux Tory. Pablo stares at me as if I'm his ruby mine. Belinda goes to buy disposable cameras but I bet she is meeting Lowell in Tony's van. When I tell strangers that I model, they imagine me on a catwalk, a stubbled apocalypse of sweat and sizzle. *Better the devil you know* said my mother, *better*. Why? Pablo is finished—for tonight. We look at the tiara we call *city*.

Three Vaqueros

1. Gustavo's Search

"Be a God: Gdlkg, Masc, in Great Shape,
Wealthy, a Genius & Free to Travel the World."[1]

Secret[2] alarm clock in my jock, I've stopped sleeping with women,[3] dreaming next to them. I made elephant[4] babies in last night's dream. A rose hurts my bed; your rival? Have you ever wanted a statue[5] on a mountain to become flesh and bones? The dead walk the night around my house. I sleep naked[6] during thunderstorms. I'm a shoplifter for love, in gladiator underwear.[7] Hangovers are[8] badly named. They're exhausted search parties. Where are you? Who am I wearing the clothes of your sweat? The world of your body is the best of souvenirs, hairy map of hope.

1. If I exist, perhaps you do too. Isn't it funny how Jewish and Catholic men in most of America are cut? I've done my own scientific survey.

2. This is a big world and I have a big heart (among other things).

3. It's for Samson and Hercules that I buy my *International Male* pouches.

4. India, I love your foods and fornicating gods.

5. Washington DC is filled with monuments of public American erections.

6. If you are a God, then save the body and soul of Frankenstein's bastard child—me.

7. Does Judas seem in love with God himself?

8. I've seen *Hans: Innocent Nazi During Nine Naughty Nights*. Fascism loves its cameras.

2. Manuel's Personal Ad

I'm a muscular[1] Renaissance man, a red thing in a boxer with hearts that only bleed in the washer. Wishes to meat you. The blue Paris of Picasso hasn't yet evaporated: it's there on my tongue. How can I not honor a nation that would keep a circumcised Eiffel Tower for themselves while sending us a drag queen, the Statue of Liberty? Prefers to be melancholic á la Henry James in a vanished Italy. Silly habit of watching CNN, Roadrunner[2] and mirrored-self. Be true to Hegelian hurricane forces that shape pubic and public[3] histories. Two-bearded. Reared in Venice and gym member in Venice, CA when younger (I'm spiritually as old as Adam[4] but less virtuous in virtual orgies). Confesses[5] nothing. Cuddles, huddles.[6] I'm in the middle of the beginning of my life. Why are you so late meeting me?

1. The body is the foam's spirit, or so it seems. Semen and sweat are the body's version of making martinis.

2. Why is it that in all the cartoons that no animals have genitals? I've looked through the Abstracts of Dissertations and nothing on this subject. Shall eunuchs inherit the Earth? Is Bam-Bam of Bedrock in the tradition of Einstein and not Alexander the Great?

3. In Shakespeare's *The Tempest*, the anonymous sailors shipwrecked with the stars of the play are left to write their autobiographies on sand, water and air. T.S. Eliot doesn't like "sweat," but he never did understand that to go public and stink is to invest in a garden of your own sweet labor.

4. I buy porno magazines just to do comparative shopping.

5. I do keep a diary, or dream's graveyard; I always write wearing white underwear, a Cubs baseball cap on before pictures of men in secret beards. Prefer to be on top but love to fall from grace and be your bottom on special holidays.

6. There's a waterfall in my head and it flows toward your desert places. Last night I dreamed of wolves trapped in attics.

3. Bethesda Ken to Silver Spring Samuel

I look good in whiskey boots.[1] FYI, dude: I'm a flutist. I have no short wish list. I worry about Whistler's father[2]; what's art about anyway? Today is my favorite past. The last shall be first is a fun sex position. Houseplants need no epitaphs,[3] agree? I love sports with choreographed[4] aches. I can and will dance just for you in my Tom Cruise bone-white underwear.[5]

1. An Irish piano player, to me, is a philosopher, handsome in the halo of his country's tragic sexual relationship with England.

2. If Adam was naked, then so must have been God. Buddha also abandoned his newborn. I prefer to worship you.

3. Gay men shall be known by inoffensive obituaries. There are too many seamless AIDS quilt panels with rainbows, smiling roses and unicorns fleeing discos.

4. A dream: thunderstorms kept us in bed and we carved ships for the dead out of silver clouds.

5. Is there a more shinier uniform than semen?

Why Jaimie Won't Join the Gay Softball Team

I used to be a macho-wannabe who was once thrown off the pitcher's mound (Hola, Freud? Lacan?). I remember crying in the shower and a teammate, who had a future as a pro, laughed at me: *you've got a mind, friend, because to me a baseball is just about a ball. For you it's a bird, a comet, an iceball from Thor and I don't know how to help you not think.* In the locker room, few of us looked at each other's false revelations. In friends' missing parents' basements, I kissed girls first, then girls and boys, then men. There is no straight line in nature, according to my public school education. I got tired of sports, of something ancient in us demanding wars without end, of adrenaline's self-love. To find yourself at 15 means to lose yourself, if you're lucky. I soon wore black eyes like love letters from the Fates.

How Oscar Became a Warrior

My old man is young at heart. Until the end of time, he's the cocksman of King Arthur's court. I follow Father up to the attic where he pulls at a drawer and elbows me in the right eye; it's a gift of stars (the cartoons have it right with stars and moons circling an injured head). My old man rocks me in his arms while telling me of baseball teams that won with the help of his prayers. We will never be closer than this, I realized even then. We stepped down from the attic, Father to his unraveling women and me to my body hair's clumsiness.

■ ■ ■

I lie to God; Father is not really dead. Easter confessions are supposed to be half-wishes. The world changes without a second thought: red tulips sprout on rooftops; fish reveal their wings and nest in trees; whiskey puts on dress pants and courts abandon churches. I return home wearing the tuxedo of dust so easily lent by the backroads where we hide from the calendar.

Father calls me out of the blue and God is no longer omnipotent. I look guilty of something or guilty of nothing. In my secret world: knives are slipped under soldiers' pillows; swans are cooked for funerals of terrorists without causes; morticians have casting couches.

"Father, what do you want?"

Drinks, of course. I turned around and head into town, my head like a lightbulb in a psychic's house ever about to burst, but not yet. Maybe never, maybe soon.

■ ■ ■

Father wants to spend our Saturdays swimming in an indoor pool. I haven't been a virgin for a week, and secrets tend to glow under one's skin. It's a strange pool, one in which you have to rent bathing suits, where old men float like seaweed, where there are rules:

1. Strip.
2. Shower.
3. Suit up.
4. Shower again.
5. Swim.
6. Shower, suit off.

And on the 7th day, Neptune rested.

I undress, hurry past Father who is talking while naked to a new friend about women: "as long as she can cook when you're hungry." I feel sick to my stomach. In the shower, I have to strip—is it a *real* law?—and so I turn my back to the graying men in the locker room. Father nudges a man next to him, "That's my son. I gave him that dick." They laugh and I fight my impulse to run. I join in the laughter. Because I no longer have the gift and grace of a boy's bones, flight is impossible. I laugh louder than everyone else.

■ ■ ■

Father's yearly visit to Mother's grave is less and less the spectacle: no DUI tickets, no animals twisted out of condoms and released to the encroaching nunnery, no blackouts while driving. And his new women come along, but wait at the mall for Father to pay respect to someone he never respected while she lived. Now, Mother is his angel, and that's that.

■ ■ ■

My Father's latest mistress asks me if I'm gay. Did Father put her up to this? He is buying cigarettes out of the gas station's men's room's machine.

"It's OK if you are because my hairdresser is and he is an angel. Who cares that he wears a fur coat on the 4th of July?"

At the restaurant, I order French toast to keep them guessing about my sexuality.

■ ■ ■

Father likes my fiancée's meatloaf. "Good hips for babies too."

She rushes off to do dishes while Father and I smoke on the porch. A shooting star. "God can't hold his semen too well. Can you?" I hear a dish full of colors breaking.

Father goes inside and uses the phone. After the breakup, I learn he called a mistress visiting the Philippines, sure that my fiancée would be an ex soon and not expect him to pay for the call. She never does. I vow that he will never meet any of my men because I can't figure out my type yet, what attracts me to a carpenter instead of a filmmaker. Patterns demand a large sample base.

■ ■ ■

Father thinks I think too much and when am I going to be caught fucking? He throws my *Flowers of Evil* out of the car window. "And learn how to drive a stick, like a man, a worker."

Years later, he asks me to read Asian brides ads to him and he praises my voice for its "poetry." Tenderness isn't for the tender-hearted.

■ ■ ■

Father said not to bring Jason over anymore. He swore Jason had a boner last time while talking to me of some homework. Father reminded me that I wasn't handsome, that the hounds of hell do eat what meat they can, even me. I hit Father for the first time and last time in my life. He wore that black eye like a betrayal, a medal of sorts; he got plenty of free drinks at *DaVinci's*.

Jason came over and told me he loved me, but I was a business major then. Once, Jason was there when Father came home drunk and they ended up talking for hours about the power of positive thinking. I stopped inviting Jason over because he was the son my Father really wanted, always praising him for this, that, anything. Jason even talked Father into calling Little Richard a "pioneer."

■ ■ ■

Father threw his boots on the dining room table: "What the hell is going on? Look! The heels are worn out. Like I've been water-skiing day and night. To hell, maybe. I might fall backwards, like a drunk. Sure, I drink, but I want credit when I'm sober. Fuck, new boots cost more than new balls. I'm going to die owing money, and bill collectors will smell my blood inside you."

■ ■ ■

I walk into your bedroom, Father, and you're trying to fly by sinking inside a naked woman. You both can't stop from laughing. I don't know what to do. You order me to go out and buy some beer. I'm only 13 goddamn years old.

José Midnight

How young we were among the sexless scarecrows. I had ambitious sideburns that were too brilliant for any narrative. José Midnight, I was. I still am, but the tragedy of getting older is that you are less mysterious to yourself. I shared rhythmic razors with tango amigos because that was a way of not talking about what we did. Grinning into the fogging mirror without guilt, we fought hard to remain boys. It was easy to wear a simple nudity—what with the shaggy crows waiting for us in America's heartland, while we circled each other around plain but eloquent motel beds. Christian truckers would stir the still air with their haste and there we were, fumbling friends laughing at a fake-wood television bolted to the stained wall. *Scarecrows like us don't get crucified. Get it up two or three times.* Things don't have to add up and they never do, *es verdad.* It's not natural when everything ends up a perfect zero. José people still call me, but Midnight was the name I gave myself, that I earned.

Gonzalo's Outburst

So? My brother's a faggot. But why does he have to love a white man? He's the enemy in and out of bed. It doesn't fucking matter whose bed. Whose bed isn't a country? He's a good kid. His new goatee can't hide it, deny it, destroy the years with us, *la raza*. Fuck you—my brother wouldn't kiss you if you were the last ride out of sobriety, *me entiendes*? Blood is blood. Not the fake blood of wine in the church every Sunday. You spill his and I bill you. Take it back. He's one of us, almost. There's no leg up in this country for all of us. A white man, shit. White. Name is Chip or Chance or the Cha-Cha-Cha Lover Man. Some name like that. My brother looks happy. Promises never to wear a dress. Not even for Halloween. It's called Devil's Milk for a reason. What men have to spill, stupid, you know? I had to tell someone. Not God. This is his joke. To punish me for sleeping with white, white, white women. That's my brother, the one who sailed paper boats with me in the toilet. Locked in there while Mami was busy being a breadwinner. She called men her manna. If we see my brother and his white man, leave them alone. In the public they got to look like friends, like us, legal, and they're under my protection? Got it? Like it or not, they're vaqueros because civilization hates them too.

Blonde under the Influence of Vodka

So Alfredo is leaving me for Antonio. That means Cordero has to bunk up with his ex, Esteban who is dating this bisexual and bicultural man, Mr. Boots. Mr. Boots really wants Augusto who is in heat over Miguel whose twin brother Guillermo is supposed to be obsessed with me (Seeing is believing and so show me el dinero). I could make Alfredo jealous by sleeping with Guillermo who is easily ten years younger than both of us. I could also go on a diet and date lots of men who may exist outside of the pages of *GQ* or *International Male* underwear catalogues. I work for Mr. Boots whose lust for Esteban is not necessarily exclusive, but then Ignacio—my office mate—might think me a slut and I care what Ignacio thinks because he's the only one who deserves to end up in heaven and might someday save our sorry asses from hell. That's because Ignacio is Cordero's first ex which makes him an automatic saint. I watch Alfredo pack and I wonder what Antonio can possibly do for him that I don't. Ten minutes later it's Miguel calling me and I make him climb the fire escape. I'm filled with hope as Miguel presses against me. Augusto pounds and pounds on the door. Some neighbor calls the police and they don't believe our tale of love for what does the law know about passion without violence? I refuse to press charges. I motion for Augusto to come in and Miguel takes off his shirt, a little tenderness for the masses. The three of us sit in the living room. Attention goes to the bottle of vodka, how little of it remains.

Fernando and Friends in Funkytown

LITTLE JAKE:

Here are some rules learned from the school of hard knocks, hola? It's me and I'm knocking, listen: don't dance near me. Disco rules. Steal drinks, but only when they're full. Don't talk to anyone about your idea that since Narcissus didn't know he was in love with himself that he wasn't in love with himself. It sounds like you have your own place. What are you waiting for?

STEVE:

Nick won't stop wearing his James Dean's hand-me-downs: T-shirt, jeans, tattoos. I comfort him after his third rejection to boogie oogie oogie. *Rockafellah Cinderellah* is jumping, but Nicky is stuck brooding; it's what he knows best. He is suddenly with a Hitler-Youth-wannabe on the dance floor: they are erotic mime artists. Maybe I should go bottle-blonde brash. Nick buys me a drink, "Whew, he didn't have your brains." But he had him for I can see what time it is in his tight jeans, the compass that points to the nearest bed. A man is more than his cock except when he isn't dancing with you. This is no musical. The rhythm predicts the past with amazing accuracy.

BUZZ:

Every song is his favorite, and he is out there but can't find the edge, can't fall off the Earth: no matter the jump, the holler, the one-to-one's. He's the last one off the floor, and the first to disappear—with whom? Without him, we'd be gossiping about each other—but about what?

SHADOW DANCER:

The night that Andy Gibb died, I was breaking up with my fiancée from Los Angeles because she was too possessive about me having a boyfriend and so the three of us met in the park with scary seagull statues and hugged, the shadow boxer was dead and so young, and we weren't, fucking American tragedy, not us, not yet, and my boyfriend kissed me in front of my ex-fiancée of two hours and she knew what he wanted, but no volcano that night, no lava revenge, for Andy was dead, and the three of us sat on top of a black mountain in Utah thinking of blood and water and the vodka my boyfriend brought along, mine until his honeymoon one year later with a woman that pleased his Mormon parents and I saw that more and more adults were going to the disco, and that I was indistinguishable from them, and I knew Andy Gibb's resurrection wasn't to be in my lifetime, and so without a woman or a man, I danced to prove that I wasn't also dead.

FERNANDO:

Historians gather in expensive hotels to tell of their copyrighted versions of disco, the life. Expansive metaphors will attempt to explain mindlessness at the crossroads of passion and fashion. We, the masses, were massive: clones, alone, bony in our beauty, stoned, groaning towards moans, our bodies deboning history. Historians, in their debts to epistemological models of the past, will pay us their highest compliment: *they were so young in a young America*.

The Blackie Soto Mystery Series

for Borges and Rechy

YOU WILL NOT WANT TO MISS EVEN ONE OF THESE EXCITING MYSTERIES. BLACKIE SOTO AND HIS AMIGOS, EVA AND JACOB, SEEM TO HAVE ADVENTURES EVERYWHERE THEY GO. WHILE SEARCHING FOR A BOYFRIEND, BLACKIE DISCOVERS THAT HE HAS A TALENT TO BRING CRIMINALS TO JUSTICE!

1. *The Invisible Matador:* Blackie Soto stumbles into a mystery when he is mistaken for a Go-Go Boy and is given a password that leads him into secret gay clubs to seek the Invisible Matador, a lost heir with legendary powers of danger and seduction.

2. *The Mystery of The Black Mirror:* Blackie housesits for a famous detective and discovers a mirror in the attic that has been painted black. Is the handsome neighbor, Miguel Santos, a love match or a spy?

3. *The Haunted Sandcastle:* Blackie's time by the sea is disrupted by the discovery of a rowboat that is empty, but for a journal. The amigos cleverly find a sexy and missing scientist, but only to find that they are all trapped on a sinking boat!

4. *The Burning Books Mystery:* Eva invites Blackie and Jacob for a vacation on a houseboat in the West. A young man with amnesia becomes their guest who keeps referring to "the burning books." Blackie tries not to fall in love with the possible forger.

5. *Ghosts on Film:* Jacob auditions for a Hollywood film and invites Blackie and Eva to join him. The arrest of the film's director for murder leads to intrigue as Blackie follow clues through studio lots, mansions and a haunted nude beach.

6. *The Clue of the White Crow:* Blackie is the understudy for a talented actor who has the tattoo of a white crow on his back. Jacob and Eva are jealous of the new friendship, but join Blackie as he faces

international assassins. A weekend in Palm Springs proves to be full of dangers and an unexpected rescuer.

7. *The Map in the Monastery:* A young priest seeks Blackie's help when a nearby monastery is suddenly haunted. Danger stalks the young detective as he learns that sometimes it is best to leave secrets alone. He finds himself running naked down a maze to escape an evil he has never encountered before.

8. *The Secret of the Red Room:* What is the connection between a series of bank robberies and the red room in the carriage house Blackie has moved into? The theft of a portrait leads Blackie to a shattered love affair between two men that only he can help mend.

9. *When the Moon Is on Fire:* A headshot session is interrupted by thugs demanding Blackie's friend, Jacob, turn over all his recent photographs. Soon, the two amigos are plunged into a mystery at a mansion's private chapel and at an adult bookstore fronting for a dangerous cult.

THE BLACKIE SOTO MYSTERY SERIES IS FOR EVERYONE WHO LIKES ADVENTURES AND FALLING IN LOVE. YOU'LL BE GLAD THAT WE GAVE YOU THIS CLUE TO FIND THIS SERIES! TELL YOUR BEST FRIENDS, BOYFRIENDS AND EVEN YOUR EX-LOVERS! SOME SECRETS ARE BEST WHEN THEY ARE SHARED!

Ricardo Ruiz

I wasn't afraid of God until Papi told me that God had a great left hook.

The expression "glass chin" fills me with terror, to this very day.

Only in Alice's Wonderland is it possible for me to shatter and then to be easily put together again without scars à la Frankenstein's monster.

I met a man who spent six months in a submarine and he said he'd be killed-off if he told anyone any details about his life inside a eggshell, at the bottom of the deep blue sea sea sea.

Sí, he gave me a copy of *Dante's Inferno*.

A code.

A clue?

I got to know him better and better until he confessed to me that he was obsessed with movies with the word "last" in it: *Last Metro, Last Exit to Brooklyn*, *Last of the Mohicans*, *Last Angry Man*, *Last Days of Pompeii*, *Last Emperor*, *Last Year at Marienbad*, *Last Time I Saw Paris*, *Last Picture Show*, *Last Temptation of Christ*.

And the strange thing is that he never went to see the *Last Tango in Paris* because he hated musicals.

I love the wrong man if he is everything I don't want.

There are many paths to Machu Picchu.

I've always known that some people don't have the talent to bribe Vanna White for a vowel.

A, E, I, O and U and sometimes Y seem to know where the red-light districts are and how to fuck themselves into sentences that make sense even as they deny the senses.

Every man—straight or gay or bisexual (I almost say "bisecting" which is almost the same thing, no?)—falls in love, trips into love, catches love.

Wouldn't that be a perfect slogan for a seafood chain or an aggressive campaign to sell jocks to every living American?

Catch yourself!

Once, I fell in love with un Cubano and he said that my genitals weighed more than the *Collected Poems of Lorca* did.

So you know what I did, of course.

I bought the *Collected Poems of Lorca* and weighed it. It was tricky to weigh my genitals.

Soft.

Hard.

Does extra blood down there add to my body weight?

I told el Cubano what I did and he laughed at me because he had been talking about the idea of my genitals, "Metaphysical, my physical angel."

So I made him step on the scales and weigh himself.

I insisted that he take off his clothes.

168 pounds.

"Some of it is muscle, Ricardo."

"I only care about one muscle right now."

So I helped el Cubano think about me, think about a part of me.

The scale moved slightly.

Probably because I was trying my best to make him tremble.

Some earthquakes are personal.

It didn't prove anything, but we were so hot and facts only confuse fucking when it's just about fucking.

One drunk morning I threw the scale out of my living room toward the dead face of the moon still in the sky.

It was a gesture of some kind, for a reason so quickly unimportant.

I turned *MTV* on right after my amateur shot-put act, just to watch the sizzle of ideas, the foam of images, the sweat of thought.

El Cubano and I were no longer in love.

I've met this Mexican.

He lip-synchs to Gloria Estefan better than Gloria Estefan does.

Isn't it easy to be a star these days?

Politicians are stars because they have either scandals or scandalous ideas.

I hated President Bush because I was afraid of him; blame my politics on my survival instincts.

His last name was Bush and only a few dared laugh at that.

No, push in the bush.

No, a democrat in the hand is worth two in the bush.

No, burning bush.

I learned one thing from my father: hands wearing brass knuckles don't do knock-knock jokes.

The CIA stands for cigars—inside—your—ass.

Look, the men next door are outside in just jocks and they're smashing their lawn furniture.

Sssh, garbage trucks are singing.

Yesterday, I dreamt of an angel whose tears could cure my friends of AIDS.

It was kind of a postmodern-Gepetto's Pinocchio world and I plucked feather after feather.

The angel cried into a thimble.

More feathers, more thimbles.

Friends were injecting themselves in every vein they could thump into surfacing: thighs, arms, neck, armpit, wrist, toes.

The angel became human and suffered our wrath for his late arrival.

We had been cured in our bodies, inside our private privates.

We turned the moon into a disco ball.

I think Hell is a bar that has a jukebox that swallows all of your coins but never plays a song.

When a professor asked me what I might imagine as the "love theme from *Lysistrata*" I offered Santana's "Black Magic Woman."

Sure, I got scars.

In some bars, they make me a celebrity.

Much of this world is invisible, though.

Sometimes I have sex because I can discreetly cry through my sex.

Not very smart.

But the male crotch is stupid and designed like some wooden leg, a lightning rod, a fishing rod.

It isn't the perfect model for the Universe, according to quantum physics; nor is the asshole a black hole, except in Russian poetry.

I believe that the human soul is merely the food for our physical bodies.

Look at the palms of my hands.

Look closely I say aloud to the lover that has yet to exist in my orgasm.

Are they empty?

These orchids of air are for you, love, even though we may never meet.

My words in your eyes, on your tongue, in your ears may be the closest chance that you and I will have to make love together, this lifetime.

Paco's Chicago Weekend

Giant men in underwear stare from the sides of unimaginative busses.
Their white triangles of hope is a contrast to the darkening streets.
These hairless ghosts mock me in my winter coat, a secret Latino
under gloves, hat, scarf. The intersections of their legs at the street
intersections remind me of the sea in Neruda's blessed seizures.
Why isn't all of this planet home for everyone? Noon, I must hide from
you, or else you might be dismayed by my plainness (not Sarah, not
tall). School children crowd the Art Institute with their laughter over
a naked man hugging a dog which may be dead: "His balls look like
apples!" The man's? I understand fleeing Eden, the need for poor
man's theater. Handsome men rush by; flesh can do much with its
limited palette. In a store window, a frightened Minsk sailor is used to
sell cuff links. A personal ad: "seeking kingdom come." Not clever, but
honest. The poet who works the hotel desk says there are no "decent"
Bloody Marys in this neighborhood. On TV: Manuel, the male stripper,
says he shakes his sexy tambourine to get through law school.
Loneliness is the one language we all speak fluently.

Carlos Begins His Quest

I took my neighbor Estrella to the 8th grade dance and right in the middle of a boring Donna Summers medley a boy nicknamed Rio came and just started dancing with us. Rio was wearing tight black jeans and a shiny shirt with dark stains under his armpits as if he couldn't control his body's liquids. He put his arms around Estrella and me. We turned in a circle and laughed as if drunk but only from the wine of our bodies. A slow song came on and I didn't know what to do. I wanted to walk away, but Rio kept his arms around us. People watched, shocked to see three people slow dancing together. Estrella threw her head back and laughed. I was amazed by the transformation on her face: she was beautiful because she was suddenly in love, or in lust, or both. Rio vanished to smoke a mysterious cigarette under the ashy stars. Later, by the doorstep, Estrella's giggling brought me back to my senses as she sang, "I guess I have competition." I pretended she was crazy and even kissed her, but then apologized for always being just un hermanito. "A brother can be a very good thing," she smiled. I crossed the wet lawn and hid in my silent bathroom. "But would a brother steal his sister's boyfriend?"

Eduardo, Hovering

He is just a trick, a Saturday night special that wasn't that special, but isn't it easier going through the express line at *Treasure Island* than the regular line? In other words, desperate measures for desperate pleasures. The stranger takes a shower that allows me the beginning of my own routines: birdseed, birdseed, birdseed. The birds of Ohio don't seem very independent at all.

The trick finds me stepping out of his spare room. I slam the pouting door. He is bragging about his youth while troubling my Martha Stewart sunset-in-Taos towel; he's a Tarzan with a voter's card and presumably good credit. And he wears that grin that he somehow has smuggled into my Old West End truffle of a rented perch. He is trouble offering me his suitcase of beauty, youth and questions that are always looking for a sugar daddy to bury.

"I don't make breakfast even for myself," I say slowly.

"I only get hungry when I'm hungry."

"You're dripping on my scarred hardwood floor," I say just to get him dressed and pressed into a taxi. He turns around and I'm sad that we don't have nine lives, that Miss Cleo will never become a historical psychic like Nostradamus, that I don't have a personal trainer, that Toledo's Mexican restaurants are either humble or humiliated.

Just as he was about to leave, he hears them.

Them.

He turns around in amazement and there's a question (a beautiful one, of course) he raises with his *GQ* eyebrows. I don't know what to say and that's actually amazing since I'm practically everyone's ghost writer. God, so many people ask me to write their commitment vows, wedding toasts, addresses to the school board asking merely for more money for chalk. He takes one step forward and I say to myself, I will not fall in love after he leaves.

"I hear birds?"

"I have a few."

"Can I see?"

There are times in one's life that others take over the party meant to spotlight your new tan lines. It's why I've never allowed my palms to be read whether the gypsy is real or a fake. My trick in a white towel is not a ghost. He opens the door to my spare room and steps back, overwhelmed by my surprise. He sees my secret: bird cage after bird cage after bird cage after bird cage. I keep birds. And they keep me. It's a room with wings.

He looks around, "The neighbors downstairs must think you are plucking angels." He then says *holy shit*, but I think he is sincere.

"And I haven't seen a romantic like you in a long time," he says, still in that towel trying to be a flag.

"I don't believe in the angels that don't visit us everyday," I say. I do say that much.

"You are interesting because you have secrets," he grins. I fall in love. The curse goes for one more ride around the block. His towel falls off, but why am I feeling more naked than this stranger actually is?

Ernesto's Secret Music, Or How to Change Class

A peaceful day after disconnecting the phone so that the bill collectors of my late payment for an emergency room "visit" will stop using my Christian name as if theirs to misuse. Fallen trees look like alphabets in books written by children: slanted L's and beheaded W's. "It's green for February," says a neighbor waiting for his high school son to come home from a college math class.

■ ■ ■

What does distinguish the human voice from the wind? Monks in Portugal chant their way across space and time to become my ear's furniture even as a storm threatens to huff and puff away my clean and well-lit place. A cello solo denies the geography of my grief for sound does not know that the metaphysical is old-fashioned. I'm not old enough to have these many names of dead friends in my phone book. I don't dare cross them out, refusing to aid Death in any way. Wind rolls garbage cans down the road, a terrible parade of loud, but invisible, forces.

■ ■ ■

Curtains in the empty room flutter. There is a bird trapped in here. I show it the sky in the mirrored ceiling. It is time to leave, abandon without pause. Driving out of town, I marvel at the tragedies that force musicians to hock their instruments. I return to the house. The bird is still there so I open all the doors and windows until the secret music that is my past is released into the night. I search the radio for balm.

■ ■ ■

Music has always been better than sex, that's how wise we were and are. We, the black-clothed, cousins to the Void, loved discos because they were messy and muddy visions in our vilest crotches. It's false that men all look alike when naked. Adam wasn't a cookie-cutter miracle. In groups, we jumped from our skin into choreographed sins, what the suburbs honored as "youth." Amnesia was the god of dawn. How religious we felt in taxis that hurried us toward strange gods.

■ ■ ■

A Russian Romeo and Romeo make love in a nocturne, music for the insomniacs between San Juan and Señor Sandman. These limbless lovers crash against each other, my furniture, ears. "Your beauty brightens the world." No, that's Shelley, poet who is still too ethereal, even for the Internet. There are pick-up clubs east of here: Lucky's, Lola's Lounge, Loose Change. Romeo, it isn't the nightingale, so stay with your wife. What you hear is me reading Marx and Engels aloud: "The Communists have no need to introduce free love; it has existed almost from time immemorial."

Secret Rome

(a farewell to Italo Calvino)

—Ciao! Come ti chiami?
—Io? Mi chiamo Pauolo.
E tu?
—Arrivederci, a pid tardi.
—Come ti chiami?
—Pauolo, a presto.
—Si, fra cinque minuti.

—Hi! What's your name?
—Me? My name is Pauolo.
And you?
—Goodbye, see you later.
—What's your name?
—See you soon, Pauolo.
—Yes, in five minutes.

The two men can no longer be strangers to each other. Pauolo regrets that he is in his business suit because it doesn't show off his basket. Still, to raise money for a film requires one to dress like a dead man. The stranger buys his cigarettes and the two men look at each other.

—Un belgioco dura poco.
—Scusa, Pauolo?
—Si, Emilio?
—La gente va in giro per i drammi.
—Abito con un cane.
—Pauolo, non ho figli.

—Fun doesn't last long.
—Excuse me, Pauolo?
—Yes, Emilio?
—People go in circles for
dramas.
—I live with a dog.
—Pauolo, I don't have
children.

Emilio jumps out of their unexpected shared bed and leaves. He has left his underwear behind. Must he always be in love? Pauolo is looking out of the window, but can't see Emilio grinning in front of his own doorway. The lover runs through the street for wine, roses and a bottle of wine shaped like a boot. Emilio knows that money at the fundraiser last night was being raised for some stupid film. Paulo greets his enthusiast with a slow kiss—many kisses for they are both terrible at math. The two men want a new heartbreak, but may not have enough time for that luxury. Making a Pope blush requires a decade or two.

—Che ora?	—What time is it?
—I mezzogiorno.	—It's midday.
—No, Emilio. I mezzanotte.	—No, Emilio. It's midnight.
—Pauolo, ho paura de filosofia.	—Pauolo, I'm afraid of philosophy.

The phone rings. It's Emilio's wife, Gabriele. He talks to her in the bathroom, the phone cord all stretched out. Pauolo stands naked in the balcony, a revelation for a non-believing city. The dancer that gets tired might as well cut off his feet. He hears his new lover stumble about in his suddenly articulate apartment. It is the night of a decision. Emilio calls him softly into the bedroom.

—Pauolo, ho paura de filosofia.	—Pauolo, I'm afraid of philosophy.

The Right José

Joe has returned to his name, José. He is embarrassed he can't talk in Spanish to Julio who finds José unsure about entering the jumping club.

There are worse things, José. You could be dead. Or straight. I hear that funeral homes are full of pervs which I find cool. Dead and still sexy, why it's James Dean as king of the world. Not like in *Titanic*. Although, the hope that the heart goes on is pretty ancient. I'm going in. Male thing to say, no, me comprendes? Pues, hermanito, can I call you little brother even if you're older? You're handsome in a kind of Long Island thug way. I can picture you thumbing houses and healing windows. No, I'm sober. For a little while. I've spread my cards on the table before and they never win the raffle. Mixed metaphors interest me because sleight-of-hand-tricks are not that sleight. The club is full of men who want to undress someone, a quarterback in a ten cent town. One lover called me Juky. No, I said, Julio, Julio. July I love your knees. Each scar is a book I mean to write but, José, writing is more handsome as sperm, ese? Pirates can be hip soon, you? This year the hot thing is low riders with PhDs. Seasons are inventions of the seasoned. And dicks have amnesia, I know that for a fact. So just rush into this mansion of music and aspire. What's wrong with that? The end of the world might happen any moment and without lubricant. We'll go in together so it looks like I'm kept. Good for my god and country, both of them ex-es. Do you think I haven't wanted to be a screenwriter? Let's go in. Maybe I'll keep you. Niño, amigo, mi alma, it's expensive to be pensive. There's music and it's never terrible to be with a liar. Maybe you think I don't think. I've been unzipped by the best. Blood never abandons the brain. Let's not go in. Let's save the cover charge and map each other instead. See, I'm younger, but I've got style. Where is all your wisdom hiding? I hope it's at intersection between fact and fantasy, what a tropical sling does for gay Caribbean cruises. Let's pretend you are as real as—como se dice—a bridge.

I would cross you. Or do you want the entire dance? Sweating in a throbbing crowd is all I want to know of joy. Then what? You'll come outside looking for me. Why do we always search for happiness when it's always right in front of your eyes. Go on, feel my chest. No, relax. That's my heart.

(José flags down the taxi and the two men jump into it, an escape. They fail to defeat or defy capitalism, but their parties become legendary.)

Paper Midnight

(Wally can't write a song for the new LP. He and his drummer, Alberto, drive around town. Wally stops at a drag bar, Lilies of the Field. They hijack the jukebox.)

It's all slash and burn. The music yearns for a birthday cake from which to pop out. One ages being a hostage negotiator, always the one who drives the train for the ghosts. *Meanwhile*: a terrible title, no? How's *Orange Weekend*? I miss just dancing, throwing myself all around like cheap luggage. The tours are getting heavy, like wet jeans. Now that I can afford underwear, I don't wear any. *Let the River Take Us Home*. Almost, but too literary, too Nashville on ecstasy. Have we ever kissed? I'm a goatee with a grotto to discover, a puppet dreaming of the callused hand. If I out myself, there are plenty of shards on which to sharpen the charms of being a stumblebum. *Sharing Razors*. No, too Goth, a go-between between God and his latest tennis partner. This place would make a great video shoot. You're right, too trendy, tactile. Bartender, more portable oceans, por favor. We've blacked out in the same waterbed, but nothing. I bought a farm just to hear the wind and nothing else. Of course, other voices creep in: trains, cars, planes, the occasional siren wearing a tiara. "Meanwhile / you've lost our passports / on a Sunday without God." Sensation isn't the brains in the family. Please say something, give me a rhythm to steal. My lyrics hurt my head: "Meanwhile / you wear nakedness / like a question."

(Wally goes to the men's room to let Alberto escape. He comes back and Alberto run his hands through Wally's hair. They are both vulnerable.)

Carlos and His Kaleidoscope

Yesterday's remains are a headache and a pocket kaleidoscope.
Pittsburgh is fogged or is this always the view from the detox floor on
which not one door has a lock. I call home but the phone is busy with
my old life. Soon I will go shopping for—oh, anything. I will have to
wear that Faustian red shirt under the suit for it's all I've brought here.
Am I giving birth to myself? No. It hurts to write this, the IV needle is
in a 45 degree angle in my right hand. It doesn't sting. Sting is what
you claim after sledding for hours, up and down hills of innocence.
In my new house in Ohio I found a sled in the basement, a "Yankee"
glider. It's worth a toast or two. The crack addict next door talks of
feeding stray cats and that Christ's Mother is more needed than Christ
who needs to kickbox to get the respect of a Saul (*when young*). I'm
on the Seventh floor, almost Heaven, but beware the wet floor—*piso*
mojado. Free puzzles try to be mysteries. I'm surprised by how I'm
allowed a phone call: "Get me out of these ass-flashing pajamas!" It's
my lover's birthday, but I've only the gifts I can steal from the hospital:
a brown comb, *Chieftain* Facial Tissues, slip-resistant footwear and a
St. Francis Hospital bag. The view looks as bulky as any paperweight.
I'm in a scene from Dickens, someone I wrote about for a B grade.
A rectal exam in a few minutes, but breakfast is here first at the
finishing line: French toast that isn't very French. I've an idea but on
checking my underwear for signs of sin, nothing. I'm not Keatsian
or very Orson Welles-among-naked-Aliens. Innocence seems an
improbable theory as I spread my ass for a Hindu doctor to praise me.
He is kind, someone for a coffee conversation, but instead he asks me
to hold my balls so they don't burden his trained hands. It's 105 days
until Christmas. I'm polite to the crack heads, the heroined, drunks
without publications. I close my door so it's closed but not sealed: it's
noisy here among the hopeful. Why did I wear a red shirt last night?
Must write *Saturday Night Fever Reunion: The Poem*. Mi Hollywood is
faithful, spectacle under the skin, where the country of the heart plays

movies against the black walls of eternity. Illusion is all that the gods can teach us of themselves. My body grows jealous and demands attendance. The doctor tells how he got divorced at Pine Ridge where my brilliant friend Adrian C. Louis shines in secret. I'm not allowed to open any window: *just in case*. Coffee, at last! Its brown body is like my own. Time for visitors, not mine. The doctor asks if my sex life has been good. I escape to the game room where men guess who is cut and who isn't. I return to my room to read a book I can recall from my memory, that black swamp. I choose *Fathers and Sons* by Turgenev. Twenty years since it made me cry at a happy hour. Francois brings the last soda before noon. Somebody down the hall's son won the Big Four, "straight too." The son? My lover drives through a storm to spring me (soon). A dream? In hours, my lover has promised that I will be eating (and drinking?) at *Majorca*, a South Side oasis. Joe, the Patient Services man, has a man with outstretched arms on his name tag: José. *Hermano!* A doctor is being stripped while I'm leaving AMA (Against Medical Advice). I slip the kaleidoscope into my pocket by my crotch where it is kept safe from the gods. I choose to play the fool who has chosen to fly under the radar except when naked.

Until Tito Is a Ghost

(He's at an empty bar, but won't talk to the bartender for that's too much of a cliché. A young Republican sits next to him. Soon, Tito is explaining magic to him.)

Sí, some kill roosters. I prefer to think I'm more abstract than that. I've never stepped aboard a houseboat, but imagine one's childhood on the water with mermen calling your name, as if we have one only. It's all about prediction, but not the dangling allowed modifiers, the KKK, flags waved up and down the Elm Street of nightmares. Dangling: that's like the secret of male anatomy. It makes sense that Las Vegas would give political refuge to bad magicians. Sense is not without its desire for an empire. Black, white, as if colors and magic don't mate. Santería is like having no language, freedom from the baggage of grammar. The idea of country was invented by non-believers, sure that maps mapped. You have eyes veiled with inherited beauty that assumes logic is still the king. Then there is us, worshipping in basements, garages, fields darker than your armpit hair. To kill a rooster is to deny a true prophet of the sun. It's not a spectacle, not Charlton Heston in *Planet of the Apes*. Tragedy is not a respecter of gods. Magic makes options seem possible, probable, portable. It doesn't mean that when I sit naked in my motel room that I mistake the remote control for a rune. No, no, to have a name means I might insist that you are real. Shit, you are real. I'm also of the religion of right now. De verdad? Have you ever had blue balls and resisted arrest? It hurts to no longer be waving hands in the air, wear dry ice, have a magician's assistant. Now, actual magic is on its knees in a Santería maybe birthed by colonial geography. It hurts that afterwards no one recognizes you off-stage and then you sacrifice a beautiful living thing, a rooster sure of its rupture. Rapture is a different thing, alchemist without a forwarding address. So which story do you want to corrupt right now? I recognize the wrong mirror. I think crows are like period marks desperate for sentences to wrong. I vote, how's that for vice? I'd vote you homecoming king, damn you to dwell in your fate line. No, I bet you work in the futures market for you belong to the future. Ah, a smile. Abracadabra is a way to trick the right brain, that hero without going on stage naked and pulling flowers out of thin air, of resurrecting the Elephant Man, of going to the Dark Side but *Stars Wars* doesn't quite understand that spirits are selfish beyond our capacity to feed them. The idea of hunger is worse than hunger. Look, nothing up my sleeves. I leave town tomorrow, return to the blur of highways inspired by the need of the national guard trekking across a dozing America. Prayer is as close to your mouth as a kiss. Let's pray.

(Tito has his souvenir and they leave the bar to kiss in an alley. It's important not to remain too anonymous.)

Manfred Must Mambo

How long can midnight wear the same mask and still be mysterious? The ruins of imported disco are the Parthenon gone wildly abstract. In the dark men's room, unexcavated boys share dirty jokes as if being satyrs is just about biology. Bored Marxist, Manfred smokes in the blind alley behind the throbbing club. He is young, tired and powerless, but for his scowling leather coat. He says to the shadows nearing him, You! My Pedro! *Pero, imposible!* His Pedro of the abs and the absolutes, of that red Aztec tattoo over a true heart, of their Enrique Iglesias Karaoke prayers. His Pedro's ghost? Why does it—he—speak to Manfred in the voice of the wind? and says nothing at all? There is much that the living do not hear. Manfred is too alone and rushes back inside the dance club, to its white noises. In this land of a thousand dances, the living prove they're not zeroes snoring inside state-purchased coffins. Only the exhausted body understands that to mourn is to mistake the past for a fact. His Pedro of the Yes and of the Sí. Here, nowhere. Neither an idea nor a dream, Manfred must mambo, skate, boogie oogie, line dance—whatever it takes to awaken his candid blood. The articulated DJ is relentless, but salvation is never paid-off with wayward sweat. Manfred leaves, stumbles down streets become shadows. Echoes urge him home to his blackout. Music spills from a house and he must mambo right there in the dead-end street. Manfred speaks to the dead, far from translators. Other men join him, determined to scare God too. A hurricane in the heart will not manifest itself as a matter of metaphysics. Manfred must mambo, must mambo, mambo. All of the men dance until dawn belongs to the living again, for a little while. They never get a thank you card for saving the world again. Manfred is determined to sleep in, but awakens because the lack of ghosts is more haunting than having ghosts. He sits up in bed, puts on his headphones and practices his own disappearing act. What is music but the art of trembling shared with the public? He can't hear the tonal storm outside of his bedroom. Manfred dances around until he finally understands what the Bible of his childhood meant that he should gird up his loins. He puts on his leather coat and makes ferocious shadows against the walls just to see how he might appear to those who will fail to prevent him from realizing Pedro's salvation. He is a storm that doesn't respect borders or gods.

ACKNOWLEDGMENTS

The following stories were previously published in magazines unafraid of the word in these dangerous times. Many thanks to the editors and readers. Also much appreciation to Patti Hartmann of University of Arizona Press for her support of the work of so many diverse writers:

"My Blue Midnights": *Blithe House Quarterly* (online). Ed. by Aldo Alvarez; reprinted in anthology, *Everything I Have Is Blue*. Ed. by Wendell Ricketts. San Francisco: Suspect Thoughts Press, 2005.

"The Europe of Their Scars": *Virgins, Guerrillas and Locas*. Ed. by Jaime Cortez. San Francisco: Cleis Press, 1999.

"Cyber Conquistadors": the section, "Electric Feasts," *Off the Rocks* (Fall 2003).

"Lois And Her Supermen": *Rosebud* (Summer 1996).

"Rat Poison: The Book of Marcus Mar": *The Alembic* (Spring 1999).

"Blood Never Rusts: A Novella in Verse" was written thanks to an artist grant from the Arts Commission of Greater Toledo and a summer research grant from the University of Toledo.

From "The Macho Dolls: Flash Fictions":

> "Bethesda Ken to Silver Spring Samuel," *580 Split* (No. 2, 2000).
>
> "Cuko Gets Nostalgic for Confusion." *MM Review* (Fall 1999).
>
> "Ernesto's Secret Music, Or How to Change Class." *Apostrophe* (No. 1, 1998).

"Fernando and Friends at Funkytown." *Eye Rhyme* (Summer 1999).

"Gustavo's Search: A Personal Ad." *Reasonable Earthquakes*. (No. 1, 1998).

"José Midnight." *Higginsville Reader* (2000).

"Lucky the Latin Lover of Lombard, Illinois." *The Prose Poem* and also *Best of the Prose Poem: An International Journal*. New York: White Pines Press, 2000.

"Ricardo Ruiz": *Eye Rhyme* (Summer 1999).

ABOUT THE AUTHOR

Rane Arroyo is a gay Latino writer who is the author of five poetry books: *Home Movies of Narcissus* (University of Arizona Press); *Pale Ramón* (Zoland Books); *The Singing Shark* (Bilingual Press/Arizona State University); *Columbus's Orphan* (JVC Press); and *The Portable Famine* (BkMk Press/University of Missouri-Kansas City).

Arroyo was born in Chicago and began his writing career as a performance artist. He performed his own work in art galleries throughout Chicago and fell in love with the writing aspects of his works. Although he published his first poem at the age of 14, Arroyo began seriously working on his poems in the 1980s. He also has written numerous plays that have been performed in major U.S. cities and internationally.

He has won the 2004 Gwendolyn Brooks Poetry Prize, the John Ciardi Poetry Prize for *The Portable Famine*, the prestigious 1997 Carl Sandburg Poetry Prize for his book *The Singing Shark*, and a 1997 Pushcart Prize for a poem published in *Ploughshares*. Other awards include the Stonewall Books National Chapbook Prize for *The Naked Thief*, the Sonora Review Chapbook Contest Award for *The Red Bed*, the George Houston Bass Award for play "The Amateur Virgin," and the Hart Crane Memorial Award.

He is currently a professor of Creative Writing and Literature at the University of Toledo, where he is the Director of the Creative Writing Program. He is also a poetry professor at Spalding University's Brief Residency MFA program and a board member of the Associated Writers and Writing Programs (AWP).